Daedalus Rising

The True Story of Icarus

Robert William Case

Cover Art
by Capri Brock

A Books To Believe In Publication
All Rights Reserved
Copyright 2008 by Robert William Case

No part of this book may be reproduced or transmitted in any form or by any means, electronic or mechanical, including photocopy, recording or by any information storage and retrieval system, without permission, in writing from the publisher.

Proudly Published by
Books To Believe In (a division of)
Thornton Publishing, Inc
17011 Lincoln Ave. #408
Parker, CO 80134

BooksToBelieveIn.com

Phone: 303.794.8888
Fax: 720.863.2013

Cataloging in publication data is on file with the Library of Congress

ISBN: 0-9820838-1-5

Keep on flyin'!

Robert William C——

Oct 09, 2010

Acknowledgements

The writing of this book began in the oral tradition of telling stories around a fire to a gathering of interested people. It was first told at a weekend retreat in the mountains of Colorado in the early Spring of 2006. The retreat was sponsored by the Men's Ministry of the Mile Hi Church of Denver, a great bunch of guys and miscreants who provided both the venue and the fertile soil for the sewing of the seeds of this story, telling the story that first time was one of the high points of my life.

I am grateful to every man who was part of that event and especially to Adam Chapuis, Barry Ebert, Jon Roderick and Simon Shadowlight. The power of their support and encouragement has made it all possible.

Then came the nurturing.

I have been blessed with direction and guidance from many wonderful people. My wife Marceil is a daily source of love, ideas, support, and editing skills. Tama Kieves first demonstrated to me how much I desired to write. Nick Peterson and Lynn Grasberg showed me the joy of storytelling. And my parents, Roy and Marjorie Case, who did everything they could do to create and grow a new person a long time ago.

Daedalus Rising is a story about what every man on this earth has in common with every other man. Inspiration for the writing came from countless sources, and I am grateful to them all.

Dedication

After my own children were grown
and moved into their own lives,
and I began more and more
to reflect upon our lives together,
upon what was and what might have been,
this book was written.

I dedicate it to you Lee and Ben,
in gratitude for the inspiration.

Contents

Introduction		8
1	The True Story of Icarus	14
2	The Dream	21
3	Falling	26
4	The Winds of Change	31
5	The Dark Night	38
6	The Threshold	43
7	The Voyage	49
8	The Gatekeeper	53
9	The Dreamtime	63
10	To the Palace	68
11	King Minos	77
12	Life in the Palace	81
13	Waiting for the Dream	87
14	The Foe	91
15	Confrontation	98
16	Another Leap of Faith	103
17	The Abyss	110
18	The Quest	114
19	Return to The Dreamtime	125
20	Icarus' Journey	129
21	Soaring Lessons	134
22	Down From the Mountain	139
23	Daedalus Ascending	144

24	The Encounter	148
25	The Village	151
26	Sharing the Sky	156
27	The Choice	160
28	The Gift	165
29	Taking Off	176
30	The Flight	182
31	The Return	188
Epilogue		192

Introduction

There have always been stories, myths, told in gatherings like this one. So imagine then, the warmth and the glow of a campfire on a clear night. The stars are bright, but to see their luminescence you must step back from the fire, separate from the gathering of young and old, families and friends and into the cool night air. Looking up, the brilliance in the night sky catches your breath and when you have had enough of the splendor of that vision, you step forward again into the light and warmth of the fire and the comfort of community and listen to the storyteller weaving the tale, binding everyone in the mystery.

Long ago in the earliest of times, long before time was counted the way that it is counted today, the stories that were told around ancient fires were all about struggle, the struggle to keep your belly full. In these old stories, the struggle stories, it is the strongest one or the fastest one that wins the meal or the mate or the territory and survives for another day. In that kind of environment, what mattered most is how sharp your teeth are, how quick your claws, and how well you can hunt or be hunted.

These are the stories of our ancestors and of a history that we all share. It is a mythology created by the telling and retelling of the old stories, generation after generation, forming a complex of interwoven patterns and beliefs lying deep at the very foundation of the culture. The people and places in the stories no longer exist, but the energies still survive somehow through the repetition of the stories. Each time one is retold, it is like a wave of energy, moving outward through time into the present, the splash of a stone falling into an ancient pond and

The True Story of Icarus

resonating into the present day. And the energy that is carried by these old stories, reverberates with the inevitability of struggle, the necessity of limitation and the certainty of loss.

Many of the myths that this civilization was built upon were inherited from the venerable Greeks. Their stories about gods and goddesses still survive. In their myths, it was the gods that had all the power. They did what they wanted, when they wanted, because that is what gods and goddesses did. Humans on the other hand, we'd serve and we'd struggle and we'd get by, until the gods became distracted with someone else and left us alone for awhile. From these stories what we learn about being human, about being a man or a woman is that the gods have all the fun and that winning is only for a fortunate few and not for ordinary humans. We must weep and know sorrow, because for us loss and limitation are inevitable.

Take a look at some of these old stories, the struggle stories and see if you can feel any of their influence in your own life today. What about the story of Persephone, a symbol of feminine beauty, much loved by her family and community? It is said that she was so very appealing that a god named Hades kidnapped her away from her family one day while she was out collecting flowers. He stole her away to his home in the underworld, a place where she became his very lonely and unhappy queen.

Or perhaps the story of Prometheus and its lesson about the wages of compassion, Prometheus was a titan, a lesser god in the hierarchy of his day and he noticed that humans were without fire. Feeling generous, he took fire from the gods and gave it to us, the humans, so that we too could have light and warmth. His thoughtfulness was not without its price. When Zeus, the king of the gods, learned of the gift of fire, he became very upset that Prometheus had acted without first consulting him. Some say that Zeus was overcome by in his own anger and that driven by this shadow side of his power, he punished Prometheus remorselessly for his deed. Others say that he was calm and purposeful as he chained Prometheus to the rock,

Daedalus Rising

explaining in simple and clear terms that he, Prometheus, had to be taught a lesson. And that this would help him to understand the need for corroboration, for consensus among the gods before taking that kind of independent action. However it began, the story ends with an eagle coming to the rock everyday, to feed on Prometheus' liver. Prometheus being a god, albeit a lesser one, grew a new liver during the night. Every day the eagle returned.

His unending torment serves as a lesson handed down through the centuries, that powerful gods may go to great lengths to keep the light and warmth for themselves. This myth of how humans acquired fire serves as a stark image of the inevitability of limitation and loss and the message relentlessly persists into the present day. We have even codified its lesson into our common wisdom, often explaining unfortunate and unexpected outcomes by saying, "No good deed goes unpunished."

These are two examples of how the energy of the struggle stories continue their onward progression into our present. Sometimes it is the lens through which history is perceived. Other times, the lessons are used to rationalize or justify the present, and just as surely, it can also be used to shape and influence the future. And even though it is not a heartwarming tradition, it is part of our inheritance. It is where we come from.

Perhaps the most telling image that the ancient Greeks created to symbolize what it means to be a man or what it means to be human, is the image of Sisyphus. He is a man whose face is barely visible. It cannot be seen clearly because all day long he pushes a large and heavy rock up a hillside, his head buried between his shoulders. He is anonymous. At the end of the day, he goes home to rest, but during the night, the rock slides back down to the same spot where it began the day before. Each day, Sisyphus awakens and returns to the rock, either not remembering or not caring and begins his labors once more, repeating an endless cycle of joyless work without satisfaction or celebration.

The True Story of Icarus

Have you ever felt the energy of the Sisyphus story resonating into your life, as you look ahead from one day to the next and the next? Can you feel the influence? It's out there every day in the commuter traffic of our large cities, seeping into the quality of life in our communities and our culture.

The point is that these old stories are not just footnotes in our history. They have been passed on to us and their lessons survive. It is an energy that continues to thrive into the present, fueled by the routines and habits of daily life. It's in the way we tell our own stories, about who we are and how we are choosing to live our lives. These ancient myths still shape and influence us. Like cultural DNA, the energy lies deep in our bones and we stand poised and ready to pass it along to another generation, an ancient doctrine that limitation and sorrow are the constants and that experiences of fulfillment, satisfaction or contentment can only be fleeting, at best.

It is tempting to try and ignore them, to minimize, or deny, or turn away from the old myths. But how long can such a persistent force really be ignored? The energy of the old struggle stories keeps circulating, readily accessible and showing up everyday in the video displays, newspapers and magazines that record and display modern life, enhanced by the competition between broadcasters to more vividly express the drama of our lives.

So where can you turn to hear a story that celebrates being human? A story that teaches that beauty and creativity are not just for the gods and goddesses and that we humans were born to move in the world with our own grace, dignity and vitality. Where does one turn then, to hear a story that teaches a lesson about the abundance that results from persistent effort towards a dream that is fired in the calling of the heart?

Some may be drawn elsewhere than to the history of western civilization, turning to another culture for guidance on how to be a better man or a better woman. Some may be drawn to the Native American tradition, or maybe to the warrior tradition of the Samurai, to find a different path in the search for meaning and inspiration. It is tempting sometimes to look in other places, but the energies of the past can't be left behind for long. It keeps showing up in our lives, seeping out through the cracks and the weak spots of our collective civilized character. No matter how many layers of sophistication we try to bury it under eventually it just shows up. No matter where you go, there you are.

It is natural and instinctive to want to find meaning in our history and in the history of our ancestors. So inevitably, we go there to look for meaning and guidance. But so often in searching through that history, we encounter the stories of limitation and sorrow, about the glory that comes from dying for a cause. And some of our governments invest quite a lot of time, money and energy in creating new struggle stories, in the apparent effort to reinforce the old lessons.

But we can do more than just relive an old myth. There are other possibilities. There are other models to choose from and believe in. In actuality, most of the old myths are only vignettes, pieces of stories not fully developed. It could be that the stories and their lessons are still unfinished. What if it were possible or even entertaining, to recreate and transform one of the old myths and infuse it with a different meaning. Using the power of the old myths to teach a different lesson, one more meaningful in the twenty-first century. A lesson that offers guidance about the inevitability of choice and the power of wisdom, instead of the necessity of limitation and loss. Imagine being guided by your mythology that it is better to thrive and prosper, than just to survive.

If you are a man, are you going to kidnap a woman to gain her love, like Hades did to Persephone? No. It makes no sense to use a club in order to kiss a woman. Why not choose instead to thrive and prosper? You can choose to persuade her that you have something to offer or that interests her. Why not learn to dance?

If you are a man and you want something of value from another man, are you going to use a gun and steal it? Not if you are smart. Not if you want to live and thrive without having to look over your shoulder all the time to see if someone is chasing after you. Why not just persuade the other man that you have something better and then trade.

The premise of this book is that the old myths that have come out of our past are not fully complete. In the same way, the stories of our own lives are not yet finished. Acorns must become oak trees. Kittens must become cats. What they are and what they become, is immutable. But a man or a woman becomes whole and fully human, by some combination of choice and the commitment kept to the calling of one's heart. We have the ability to influence the evolution of our lives. The only real question is what am I to be, and what journey to take in order to get there?

The true myth behind the Icarus legend is a story of how once, long ago, a father and a son answered those questions. It tells of how each one moved toward growth and fulfillment by sensing and being aware of the direction of true purpose and following its path. The weaving of this new tale demonstrates that even something as old and tired as a building block of ancient mythology can be transformed into something vital and meaningful in this twenty-first century.

The story that follows is the natural completion and unfolding of the ancient myth and its telling, a metaphor for the potential within each of us.

Chapter 1

The True Story of Icarus

> *Myths inspire the realization of the possibility of your own perfection, the fullness of your strength and the bringing of solar light into the world.*
>
> ~Joseph Campbell, The Power of Myth

Have you heard of the story of Icarus? You know the one, the old myth about the boy who flew too close to the sun on wings given to him by his father. It is a story that has been told millions of times, over thousands of years, around countless campfires and classrooms. It is one of the old stories, a struggle story. But what if, buried beneath the literal form of that ancient myth, there is a meaningful lesson about initiation and being whole and fulfilled as a man? Could it have been overlooked and lost for the last four thousand years? What if the old myth only told a small part of the tale and the true message only now revealed?

Begin there, repeating the old tale one last time and making it the starting point for a new mythology. In the original tale, Icarus was the son of Daedalus. And Daedalus was not a god. He was not even a hero like Ulysses, or Hercules. He was a man, one of us, someone who tried to do the right thing and wanted a good life for himself and his son. And he was an inventor and builder of some renown. One day, he found the inspiration to design and build wings, wings to give a man the power of flight. He set himself to these tasks and to this goal and eventually built two pair. One pair he kept for himself. The other, he gave to his son.

Now consider this for a moment. Who among us has not dreamt of flying, of soaring like an eagle through the sky? Who, as a small child, did not go out into the backyard on a warm and sunny afternoon, lift up their arms, go into a spin and lift one leg up and then the other and feel the energy, the power of rising up, up off of the earth. To know for one brief instant, what it feels like to defy gravity and soar into the sky? Take your eyes off the page for a moment and close them. Feel that small child on the warm summer afternoon, spinning around in the backyard grass with arms outstretched and remember the magnificence of that feeling of flight.

What an incredible gift for a father to give and what an incredible gift for Icarus to receive. In the old myth, Daedalus built the wings from the feathers of seabirds and wax and then, as he gave the wings to his son delivered the now classic warning, "Icarus, don't fly too high. Your wings are made of wax and they will melt in the heat, if you fly too close to the sun."

How old was Icarus? He was old enough to have the strength to fly for a long distance. He was at least well into his teenage years. So how foolish was it then, for the father to give an incredible gift like that, the gift of flight, to a teenage son and in combination with a warning that would most surely be tested? If you've ever been a teenage son or daughter, imagine what it would have been like, at the age of sixteen, to receive a gift like that from your father or your mother, or from someone much older that you cared about. What if you were given a 1969 Ford Mustang Mach 1, powered by a 289 cubic inch, V-8 engine, with a 5-speed manual transmission and a full tank of gas? Imagine yourself receiving that gift and as your father hands you the keys, he says: "Now keep it under 55 mph on the highway, 25 in a school zones and go have fun."

That's right. He actually says those words. Imagine yourself in that situation, receiving such a gift. Would you have even heard them? Probably not, but even if you did hear the words, what do you think you might have said in response? An excited utterance? A joyful scream? "Thank you very much and I'll see you later." Maybe you wouldn't have said anything. Maybe your mind was lost somewhere in a vision of you behind the wheel, driving down the main drag of the town to the awe and amazement of your friends and peers.

If you have ever been a son, then you know what must happen next. Maybe not right away, but some time in the very near future, you would find a deserted piece of asphalt somewhere and run that monster of a car. Even if you don't go looking for it, the opportunity would find you and when it did your heavy foot would not resist the irresistible attraction of the gas pedal. You would give yourself into the experience of acceleration and speed. The deepening roar of the engine, your right foot hard to the floor, the car leaping forward, shoulders forced back into the black vinyl seat, hands on the dancing wheel. All of it delicious.

At some point, you would find yourself on just the right road at just the right time and you would push that car to see just how fast it could go. You have to know this. Everyone who has ever been a son knows in their own heart that with such a gift, eventually, they would surely do exactly the one thing that their father warned them not to do.

So what else could Icarus have done? Of course, he listened to his father's words. He heard the warning and then he joyfully accepted the wings. Maybe he acknowledged the gift, maybe he even responded to the warning.

"Yes father, thank you very much, I will do just as you advise."

And then as quick as he could, he took the wings out for a test flight. He carried them up to the top of a nearby hill, mounted the wings, adjusted the pitch for maximum lift and then took a couple of test jumps into the air. Turning into the wind, he ran down the face of the hill as fast as he could and still keep his balance and then he leaped into the updraft of a steady wind. On his own weight, he dropped forward a bit, but then, just before hitting the ground, the wings caught and held and Icarus rose higher and higher, finding an uplift and soaring up and away from the earth. Gravity let go of him and Icarus learned firsthand the exhilaration, the magnificent splendor of soaring through the currents of the open air. He learned to gain elevation by facing the oncoming wind, balancing himself against it and letting it push him higher until he could glide, soaring effortlessly on outstretched wings, wherever he wanted to go. He felt so alive, his heart singing with joy, so loud and so strong that his father and the warning words were the last things on his mind.

Icarus flew and all the time he learned more and more about what he could do with the wings and the thrill of flying through the open air. The feeling of it filled his senses and he could not resist soaring longer, faster and higher. His father stayed in the lower elevations, watching. And then, after a short time or a long time or whatever time that it took, Icarus flew right into the one place that his father warned him not to go, into the sun. In its heat the wax melted, the wings broke apart and Icarus fell into the sea and was lost.

What a tragedy. And there it is again, the same old tired lesson of the old myths. The one that teaches that loss and limitation are inevitable and that it is not safe to stand out, not safe to fly, not safe to soar into the light and warmth of the sun, independent and under your own power. The old myth is not only sad, it is toxic and it is time to let it go.

What does that teach us about trying something different, or learning something new? If you listen to that myth and its lesson and you have aspirations and talents and want to grow and develop them into abilities, the message of the Icarus story can only compel compromise. What if you as a parent want to encourage your children to follow their dreams and to be all they

Daedalus Rising

can be? Then you certainly don't want to use that tired old myth as a source of inspiration. How could so bleak a story have survived for all those centuries?

And consider as well, what the old myth says about Daedalus and what it means to be a father. If Daedalus, or maybe your own father, warned his sixteen year old son that he must never ever, take that Mustang Mach 1 out to the old deserted airport on the outskirts of the city and run it to the red line, then surely he has to know, having once been a son himself, that Icarus would be drawn to that old deserted airport like a moth to a flame. Because that is what sons are born to do, they test the will of their fathers. Daedalus knew that. Or at least,he should have known it because once, not all that long ago, he would have done the same thing himself, back when he was a son. Shouldn't he have known that by warning his son not to fly too close to the sun, he might as well have sent him an invitation?

That's why the ending for the old Icarus myth just doesn't make any sense! For one thing, Daedalus had to know that he was sending Icarus out to fail and that he might even lose his life. For another, Daedalus was an inventor and creating working wings was an incredible accomplishment. It had to be his life's work. Why would a great inventor devote all that time and energy, designing and creating such a wonderful gift, only to be complicit in its destruction? A fine artist or an inventor just wouldn't do that. And a loving father wouldn't either.

Examining it closely, the old myth just doesn't make sense. It doesn't stand up under any kind of scrutiny, but somehow history has kept on repeating it anyway, for centuries.

Maybe that's not the whole story. Did anyone other than Daedalus actually see him fall? No. What we do know is that both of them had wings and both were far from land out over the sea. Daedalus was the only one, other than Icarus, who saw what happened. When everything was over, he was the one who reported what happened. He created the history. And his story grew and it was passed on and it just kept on being repeated for the next four thousand years. For some reason our culture has chosen to keep telling and retelling it, exactly the way that Daedalus wanted it to be told, the way that he wanted it to be remembered.

So what else could have been going on that day? After all, Daedalus was a clever man, someone with a gift for invention. He figured out how to design and build wings. He had to be smart enough to know, that Icarus would test both him and the wings. He would have expected it. So we don't really know what happened in the sky that day, but it is certain that the old story does not tell the whole story. The old myth that has survived all these centuries is no more than the part that Daedalus wanted told.

He could have had a completely different purpose and so the story was just a vehicle to achieve those ends. Maybe it was a cover-up, a clever ruse concealing a great mystery that has endured for thousands of years; one whose time has finally come.

Or perhaps the old myth was just a slight of hand to hide the mundane. What if on that day in the sky Icarus was acting the rebellious teenage boy and on a whim he ditched his father and ran away, or in his case swam away and headed back to the island that they launched from. Maybe Icarus didn't want to leave his home or his friends behind. Perhaps he was after his independence at any cost. Imagine then what the father might do, realizing that he was alone in the wide open sky with a fine pair of wings and nowhere else to go, except toward his own horizon.

Whatever did happen that day, there is more to the story. That much is certain. And we must accept the very real possibility that the mythology that has been passed down to us through hundreds of generations, is a subterfuge, a trick. Just imagine a deception so thorough and complete, that it became a story that grew into a myth that has endured for centuries; long after Daedalus, or Icarus, or his children, or his children's children had any interest in what really happened on that day in the sun. And what if it was intentional, a trick so thoroughly complete that it fooled all of western civilization for a few thousand years? What could Daedalus have wanted or needed to hide that much?

We know that Daedalus was a father, an inventor and a builder. But what if he was also a trickster? Then the mystery he intended to craft, is finally revealed.

Chapter 2

The Dream

He who is creative, must create himself.

~John Keats

A stand of cypress trees shaded the courtyard and the house from the heat of the day. The stone walls that shaped it were built to last, designed with a simple elegance that conveyed a sense of security and comfort. It was all very much to his liking. Daedalus did not want or need a lot of living space and his attachment to the home was grounded as much in the view as in the building itself. He had always been drawn to prominences, places where he could pause and view distant horizons. Perhaps he should have been a sailor with horizons in every direction, but that was not the way of it, at least not so far.

Each journey begins at home. It is the place we all start from. The place where we receive, from family and community, the lessons of who we are. And so it is by leaving it, that we discover our own creative influence over what we are and of what we will be. For Daedalus, home was the city of Athens.

It was part of a valley that ran along the length of a broad, mountainous peninsula projecting out into a vast blue sea. In another time, the earliest of times, the valley was known to its inhabitants by the large plateau which lay at the center. The huge rock was bounded all around by sheer walls, providing a view for miles in every direction. Over the years, it became a fortress and a citadel for anyone who claimed it and as the

Daedalus Rising

centuries passed, shepherds and farmers that lived nearby used the high place as a hub for trade and for exchanging their wares.

In Daedalus' time, the rock had become the central core of the city of Athens and on one side a broad path zigzagged up the rocky slope. At the top, it widened into a road paved with flagstones that led to the king's palace, the temples and to a few elegant homes for the important nobles. From the steps of the palace, you could look out and see far across the valley to the purple mountains that edged the plains and formed the boundaries of the kingdom.

And there was a view from the courtyard of Daedalus' home; not quite as grand but more than enough to inspire. There was even a raised platform built against the wall of the house for nights like this one, for sleeping in the cool air under a starry sky. It was a beautiful, still night and from his vantage point among the pillows and blanket, he looked out beyond the darkened space that held the sleeping city. The dark profile of the distant mountains framed the brilliance of the night sky, like a huge black bowl inverted and holding a universe of stars.

Sometime in the night the dream came, but not in the usual way. Not the kind that rises up out of one's own imagination. This one came upon him from outside of himself, stealing up on him and taking him by surprise. He was transported away so swiftly that his arms and legs and even his head, were immobilized from the force of the acceleration. Sensations of restraint and motion enveloped him, just as a mellifluous voice came to him in the dream, telling him in soothing tones to relax, that he was safe. Hearing this, he understood that he was not alone, that he had a companion with a beautiful soothing voice and they were steadily accelerating across a great distance.

"Whoever was speaking," he thought, "certainly knew the right words and just how to say them."

The tones were so soft and so peaceful, that he relaxed. Comfort filled his senses. The words were coming from a source right at the back of his head. He wanted to squirm, to move and turn his head just a little bit, to see who or what was there, that could communicate in such pure, clear tones. But he couldn't move, not at all, not even to lift a finger, not yet. But all that could wait, couldn't it? It was only a dream after all.

In that time and place, he had no will of his own. He had given it over to the voice, trusting it and the dream, choosing to follow and see where it would lead. Eventually, when he could move again, perhaps then there would be time to turn around and see whatever might be there.

And then he stopped moving. He found himself in a shadowy warm place, lit with subtle tones of yellow, red and brown. It could have been a cave but it was warm, not like anywhere he had ever been before. It was strange that his arms and legs were still immobilized, because there was nothing he could see or feel that bound him. And there was movement all around, slowly shifting shadows and Daedalus understood that he was not alone. There were many others. Still the voice accompanied him, telling him that he was safe and protected. He wanted to speak out and make some sound of his own, an announcement, some kind of acknowledgement, but his lips and tongue would not move in that way.

A yellow brown tablet appeared before his eyes and a message began to form upon its face, written in a language that he did not know or understand. The voice explained in calm, tranquil tones that the meaning of the writing was a promise, a pledge that he would be offered a wonderful gift, something so great that it could set him apart from all other men.

"What do you want from me?" asked Daedalus.

The comforting tones of the voice went on. "You have a choice. If you agree, then the pledge becomes our covenant and you will return, knowing that you are called to receive a great gift. If you say no, then you return to everything that you have grown accustomed to and without an appetite for anything more."

"What do I have to do?" he wondered.

"Just give your word, your promise Daedalus, that when the gift makes itself known, you will be willing to receive it, whenever or however that happens."

"Tell me what the gift is. How long must I wait? How will I know it when it arrives?"

"There will be signs. If you watch for them you will know and they will appear when you are ready. And until then, all of us gathered in this place will watch over you. You will have no reason to fear."

He still had questions, many of them, all of them insisting on some specific information about the gift. They rang through his head and he tried to direct them somehow to the voice. It did not respond to the specifics of his questions, but only said, "You need only be ready and willing and not turn away. You cannot be too busy or fearful, or have some other excuse. Just decide, whether you have enough trust in yourself to give your word without first having all the answers."

Still Daedalus could not move his lips to speak. His mind was turning out questions, one after another, but he knew in his heart that whatever the gift was, he wanted it. Of course he did. The voice promised a wonderful gift, one so great that it could set him apart from all other men. He felt his attraction for the gift and it was much more than longing or desire, more even than intuition and that was enough. Soon, his mind agreed.

Yes, he wanted it, whatever it was. His conscious mind took over and he thought. It would be foolish not to agree. There's nothing to lose here and everything to gain. Why wouldn't I say yes?

From inside somewhere, he felt his words of assent taking form and he projected them, fashioning his response as best he could. Holding onto those thoughts, he looked once more at the incomprehensible dark scribbles on the face of the tablet. The meaningless marks were changing into letters he recognized and they formed into words that were clear and meaningful, commemorating a contract where none had been before. He read the words making a memory of what was written.

As he read, the writing began to fade and the tablet was withdrawn. The shadows began to recede into the warm stillness of that place as his own body began the return trip, once again accelerating across a great distance. His arms, legs and head were still immobile and the voice was still there, intoning the same soothing words. Now, more than ever, he wanted to turn around and see this companion and learn how it was that his body could be held so completely still.

Then he was back in the courtyard of his home, lying tangled in his blanket and pillows. The voice was gone. His eyes were tightly shut, but he was awake. Cool air and darkness surrounded him. The sublime blend of power and kindness that had held him immobile was gone as well. He could tell that his arms and legs were his to move again, when he was ready, but he wanted only to lie in the quiet. The energy of the dream was still with him and it felt so serene to lie in the stillness and remember the flood of sensations that accompanied the dream. And what a dream it was! So vivid, like nothing he had ever experienced and Daedalus wanted to hold onto the memory of it as long as he could. He knew it all would begin to fade as soon as he started to move again and he wanted to hold onto it, to ponder it and most of all to consider the gift.

"What could it possibly be?" he asked again from the courtyard of his home.

Whatever it was, dreaming about the possibilities excited him. Soon the energy of it all was more than he could hold in. His eyes opened and he was wide awake, lying upon his bed. The same stars twinkled above him. Had he even left? He wondered and he remembered the tablet, how he had once read and understood the words with such clarity. Now he could hardly remember what was written there, but that didn't matter. He could remember his promise and the thought of it brought a smile to his face. There would be no more sleep that night.

Chapter 3

Falling

We are all artists of our lives. One day we are given a hammer with which to make sculpture, on other days we are given brushes and paints..., or paper and pencils to write with. Each day we have different tools. Therefore however difficult it may be I must accept today's small blessings...
~Paulo Coehlo

On a new moon night in the spring, a line of heavy thunderstorms swept across the valley. Early the next day, Daedalus was summoned by the King. The roof of the palace was in need of repair. This was not their first meeting, not at all. Daedalus was known in Athens as a master builder and architect, a well-earned reputation founded in the fine homes and temples that he designed and built. Many of them stood near the palace itself.

Daedalus loved his work, or perhaps more accurately, he was his work. In his community, he was the architect and builder for the king. He was known for the persistent, focused energy he brought to his projects. To Daedalus, the many accomplishments were well worth whatever other desires he might have wished for and buried under daily efforts to maintain his standing in his chosen field. Now with the approach of his middle years, he lived alone in the comfortable, eclectic house with the shady courtyard and outstanding view, built from his own design.

Perseverance and dedication to his crafts served him well, but it was not these character traits alone that brought his work to the attention of the king. Instead King Aegeus was most impressed by the originality of his ideas and by the passion that accompanied them. There were many skilled craftsmen in the city. What made Daedalus different was his ability to persuade the king and others that his ideas and designs were the best. Behind his back, there were some detractors usually competitors, who claimed that it must be some kind of charm, because his work was just not worthy of the attention it received. Others simply said that he must have a gift.

Daedalus did not pay too much attention to the critics. There was no need to, because when by himself, he could be as critical as the best of them. What kept him going was his belief in his own imagination. He knew well the ambiguity between his convictions and his doubts. It was always there. Even with the ideas that seemed so strong, there was always an uncertainty that would not resolve. Resolution came only when he acted on the ideas, embraced the doubts and moved forward anyway, in the process convincing others that they should also be saying, "Yes."

On this particular morning, Daedalus and the king toured the interior of the palace, taking a roundabout approach to the problem. Aegeus enjoyed entertaining and as they walked through the palace, he vividly described the storm of the night before. How the rain poured down, thunder roared and lightening filled the sky. It was all very exciting, right up until the huge crash of a lightening bolt striking the palace and tearing into the high roof. Then the walls of the palace shook, the sound of it roared through the floors and then echoed through the spaces of the rooms. Stone, wood beams and clay tiles were ripped apart and the rain poured into the rooms below.

Beneath the damaged area, debris and dirt piled up everywhere, brightly illuminated by blue sky and light blazing in through the hole set off by the damaged roof beams. Servants busied themselves with the mess, carrying it away piece by piece and soaking up the pools of water that lay in the low spots of the stone and tile floors. The queen joined them while Aegeus and Daedalus watched the activity and soon they were all sitting

Daedalus Rising

together, exchanging ideas about everything that needed to be done, the proper order and how long the repairs would take. They spoke with the familiarity of people who had worked together before toward a common goal.

While they talked and planned, the sun rose higher, doing the work of drying everything out, and after enough time had passed Daedalus alone, climbed onto the roof. The palace was built atop the huge rock outcrop in the center of the city and one side adjoined the edge. Along that one side; it was hundreds of feet from the roof to the rocky ground below and the view was breathtaking. Daedalus paused for a long while there and then turned, moving slowly and carefully across the face of the roof, knowing how and where to step so that the tile would not break under his weight. All the time, he looked down along his feet on the path and not out towards the edge. That direction made the roof a dizzying place.

The lightening struck one of the high corners of the roof. He made his way deliberately towards the large and raw opening that provided complete access from above, down to the water soaked rooms below.

Peering over the edge, he studied the damage for a while, imagining what it would look like when it was whole again. He decided what steps needed to be taken to make that happen. Finally, he composed a list in his head of the materials and tools. He descended from the high place in the afternoon light, returning to his workshop to assemble a crew and explain the project and the plans. It would all begin in the morning.

One of the workers was a boy named Talos, a new and eager apprentice, who decided to include a plan of his own. He wanted to prove his worth to the others and to the master builder. So he decided to rise early, earlier than anyone else and begin carrying materials and tools up onto the roof before anyone else arrived. He wanted to be noticed by the others, but especially by Daedalus.

That night it rained again, soaking into the palace roof and creating another small pond within the palace. This time the room was empty, but there was still plenty of frantic activity inside the palace. There was more thunder and lightening too, but this time in the distance, not the kind to jolt a sleeper awake in the middle of his slumber. A few hours before dawn, just as Talos rose from his bed, it stopped.

Before the sunrise, Talos was at the palace, ready to begin his work. As he climbed out onto the damp roof in the cool morning air, the sun pushed up over the eastern mountains and into the few clouds that remained from last night's storm. It promised to be a magnificent display. It even smelled good, the kind of fresh, clear morning that comes after a storm. Talos breathed it all in, he thought he could see forever in every direction.

He was energized. Youthful vigor surged through him and he bent to pick up a load of tools and roof tiles. Balancing them in his arms, he carried a load up the scaffolding and stepped out onto the roof. He moved diagonally across the steep pitch, carefully placing one foot in front of the other on the wet tile. One eye looked ahead to the place where the roof was ripped apart and the other down at his feet. He looked for and found the place on the next piece of tile that would bear his weight. It looked whole and complete and the moist surface glistened in the sunlight as he put his foot down surely, near an edge rather than the middle so as not to break it. In a continuous motion, he transferred his weight forward and to his surprise, there was a sharp crack. The tile broke apart. The broken piece fell away and his foot lost its purchase on the smooth surface. There was a clatter as the broken tile rolled and bounced down the pitch of the roof.

Talos turned his head toward the noise just long enough to watch it descend. His own body fell backwards onto the sloping side of the wet roof. He spread his arms out, freeing them from the load he carried. Pieces of tile and tools clattered onto the roof, breaking more and then starting their own long slide downhill towards the edge. He brought his forearms and hands down hard onto the steep tiled surface to break his own fall.

They did that much, but by then his own body had already begun to slide. A low moan escaped his lips.

He thwacked his feet onto the roof. He groped for a handhold, anything for his hands to grasp. He lifted his head and he looked down past his knees to see what remained of the roof. His eyes searched frantically for something to hold onto, anything, but there was nothing in reach. He flipped over onto his stomach, spreading his arms and legs in a desperate move to somehow meld himself onto the expansive surface as it slid past. But he just kept sliding. The seconds expanded, filling up the time that remained, and then he reached the edge. His hands groped toward that thin purchase in one last try to stop the fall, but there was not enough strength in his fingers and forearms to hold him and he tumbled over the side. One more time, the sky and mountains came into view and then he saw no more.

Chapter 4

The Winds of Change

There was never any more inception than there is now,
Nor any more youth or age than there is now,
And will never be any more perfection than there is now,
Now any more heaven or hell than there is now.
~Walt Whitman, Leaves of Grass

Daedalus kept himself busy. Even when he wasn't at work he was still working, thinking through his lists of things to do, checking off some items and leaving others, marking each step so that the next one could begin. In his memory, the days and weeks blended into months and years, forming a seamless pattern of well worn habits, perceptions and routines. Early on, his desire to build created the routines and habits. Then, they sustained him. Now, they defined him. At least, that was the way of it, right up until the day the boy fell from the roof. That day held a significance like no other.

The boy had not been working for him for very long. He seemed an eager youth, willing to work as hard as a young boy can, but in fact, Daedalus hardly knew him. There were many apprentices over the years and until the fall from the roof, Daedalus had not noticed anything about this one to distinguish him from any of the others. Of course, the boy's fall was an unfortunate event, a tragedy, but it didn't mean that the work should stop. Accidents happen on building sites and often times, there's no one at fault. At least, that's what Daedalus always told himself when these things happened. There would be a pause, a slight shift in the rhythm of the work and then life would go on, much the same as it always had.

The boy's mother had a different view. She was devastated by the death of her son. She could not eat. She could not sleep. She went to the workshop, looking for Daedalus. She wanted to tell someone of her grief. She wanted an explanation and hoped for some peace. That particular day Daedalus was very busy with other things. More than that, he had little interest in taking the time to see her pain or face her grief, even though he knew that he should. So the first day that she came, he gave into his own busyness and avoided her.

The second day went much the same.

The third day, she returned to the workshop. She had not slept much that night, or the night before. Instead, she turned deep into her grief, continuing the process of fermenting her pain and sadness into anger. By morning, it smoldered and burned deep inside. Just like her son before, she rose early that day, so that she could have a chance to impress herself upon the builder, before he could hide away and occupy himself with other things.

At dawn, she was right outside of the workshop. She waited, a young woman aging quickly and shrouded in black. He did not notice her at first, not until she started to move. Her path caught his attention right away. She walked directly towards him, her steps resolute, the anger palpable. Their paths would intersect and this time there was no avoiding her. He had no choice but to abruptly stop and look downward into the determined, careworn face. Without a word, her dark eyes bore into him, taking his measure. She seemed to be looking for something, tilting her head one way and then another. Then the stream of words began to flow, the tone building steadily and the emotion escalating into the torrent of furious rage, demanding to know why.

"Why was my son all alone up on that roof?" An upraised fist banged into his broad chest. Daedalus just looked at her, quizzically, but said nothing.

"Where were you, anyway?" Another fist. He took a step back, still too shocked to speak.

She advanced, angrily, following him. "Why wouldn't you talk to me yesterday?" Two more fists, another step back.

"Stop that!" he finally said.

"Or the day before?" she followed relentlessly. Another fist lashed out, but this time he stopped and pushed it away before it struck.

"What are you trying to hide?" A finger pointed and wagged in his face.

"I'm not hiding anything," as his hand grabbed at her wrist, stopping the fists. But they could not quench the fire of the rage that burned in her eyes. He had no idea what to say next. This was beyond the comfort zone of what he knew and what he had experienced. Her face was a mask of pain and sorrow. She focused all of it on him. She blamed him. All he could see, all he could feel was the anger she vented. He was not aware of the grief behind it. He did not know how to respond with understanding. Instead, he felt attacked and became defensive. Part of him wanted to find a door to close, or a wall to hide behind, but there wasn't anything like that out on the street that day. Only onlookers, seeking entertainment. The only barriers he had available to hide behind were the ones he could erect around his own heart and that is what he did.

Thus armored, he was able to find a few words, ones which seemed logical at the time and said: "I don't really know what happened, because I wasn't there. I don't know why he was out on that wet roof alone."

She did not appreciate his comments, which seemed an effort to shift the blame back to her son. She felt worse still. It fueled the anger and she escalated even further into her rage, struggling with the much larger man to free her hands, screaming, "He wouldn't have been gone up there at all, unless

Daedalus Rising

you told him to!" She wrenched one of her hands free and used it to slap and tear at his face. He released the other one in order to roughly push her away and she fell onto the ground and wept.

If Daedalus could have shown a little compassion for her grief, if he could have reached down and extended a hand to her, put an arm around her and comforted her, then things might have gone very differently. But either he couldn't do it because he didn't know how, or he wouldn't because he was too afraid. Whatever it was, he couldn't get out of his own way. Instead, he turned and walked away. She did as well, exhausted and silent, tears running down her face. She backed away from the crowd and left, taking her anger with her. It was cooler and more refined now and eager for vengeance.

She began to tell others, anyone who would listen, of her grief over the loss of her son. She told of the cowardly denials of the man responsible for his death and of the pain in her heart. As she told the story, the details began to grow and soon she was describing the suspicious nature of the boy's fall. She blamed Daedalus for not being there. She accused him of needlessly exposing her son to a danger that he had to have known about and with no one there to help. She told her story to anyone who would listen.

There were many who did.

One man that listened came forward and spoke. He was a man that Daedalus had once fired from his workshop, but he did not explain that detail to the onlookers. He was able to explain however, that he saw the master builder out on the roof of the palace the day before the boy's fall, loosening and breaking roof tiles. Seeing this, he had wondered why Daedalus would weaken the roof tiles like that, knowing that others would be walking across them in order to reach the damaged section of the roof. After that, the mother of Talos and her new friend told their stories together, whenever they could to whoever would listen and the story of the boy's fall continued to grow.

Just as Daedalus was not good at comforting a grieving mother, he was not skilled at telling his own story. When asked about the incident, he typically responded with indignation and said things like: "How could I know what happened on the roof? I wasn't even there." Or, "Of course, I didn't damage the roof. Years ago I built it." Or, "How can anyone believe that story from someone I once fired."

He just wanted the fervor to die down and go away. He couldn't or wouldn't see what was happening. He quickly grew tired of the whole business. No matter what he said, it was the same baseless questions again and again. It was demeaning. Over time, his responses became muted with growing fatigue. More than anything, he wanted to hide behind his walls, wait it out and not have to deal with it. Eventually, he hoped and repeatedly told himself, the anger and the talk against him would fade.

"This has to die down. How can it continue every day, when I have done nothing wrong?"

The mother of Talos would not let go of the anger. She blamed Daedalus. She said his silence was proof of his guilt. She told anyone who would listen and eventually she found an important nobleman who listened to her story. He was a man with a certain amount of influence in the noble house of the king and he had long coveted the home in which Daedalus lived and it's view of the city. He took up the cause of the mother of Talos, artfully turning her grief into a public issue. With his voice joining in, the incident became a political statement. In a short while, the word spread among the nobles and the people of Athens, of the need for justice for the boy.

The fall from the roof became the talk of the town. Daedalus heard himself maligned by people he had never met and did not even know. It was as if his guilt was a conclusion and he didn't even realize he had been on trial. People in the street, strangers pointed their fingers at him and glared. It was as if just by walking past, he could induce others to join into conspiracies against him. Everyone seemed to stare, wherever he went. Sometimes, they would jeer at him. Then his workmen no longer came to work. He had no new business and his existing business cancelled. He tried to go to the King and speak with him, but the King would not see him. He had become an island, alone, inside the city that was his home.

Then one day, while he walked down a street in the town, a rock hit him squarely on the shoulder. The impact of the blow twisted his body and pushed him forward just enough, that the rock that followed sailed past without hitting him. There was only the whooshing sound as it passed his ear. He looked back and could see several young boys run towards him, rocks in their hands. There was an angry crowd behind them, egging them on, yelling and cursing. There were more rocks and sticks in the air, some landing on the ground around him, others flew past. So he ran.

Many years had gone by since he had run anywhere. But he knew how. He was terrified. His legs responded and carried him away, faster than he would have believed he could go. Around one corner, then another and then he just ran. The angry mob did not follow for long. Soon the shouting grew faint. When the rocks and sticks no longer fell towards him from the sky, he finally stopped, completely out of breathe. He bent over at the waist, hands on his thighs. His chest heaved and tears filled his eyes and ran down his face. When he was able to stand up, there was a sharp pain deep in his upper thigh. The hamstring muscle, unused to such exertion, was refusing to take any weight and he bounced and hopped on his one good leg to try to lessen the pain, cursing the crowd that had driven him away and cursing his luck.

"I built this city and now you're throwing pieces of it at me."

Hurt and alone, Daedalus limped to the road that lead up the hillside to his home. He had no where else to go and when he finally made his way to the courtyard, he was exhausted. He went straight for the door. He had long forgotten the old dream, the one with the promise of a great gift. It was just as well. He would have scoffed at the idea now. All he wanted was to feel the walls of his home close in around him and to be alone. He walked up to the sturdy entryway door, opened it and entered into the dark and quiet space, sliding the bolt to ensure his seclusion. It was all he could handle at that moment. He sank into the silence and solitude, making his world as small as possible. Not since he was a little boy had he felt this way. He was exposed and very alone.

He built a fire and wrapped himself in blankets. He fed off the warmth and the light. It was so empty and cold everywhere else.

Chapter 5

The Dark Night

A man with no imagination has no wings.
~Muhammad Ali

Alone in his darkened house Daedalus stared into the depths of the few remaining coals in the fire. They were going dim and there was no other light. There was a chill in the air, everywhere except under the blanket wrapped tightly around him. On the one hand, he wanted to move, to do something, get up, pace around the room, or get more wood, do something to warm himself again; but on the other hand, it took so much effort to overcome the inertia. He felt rooted to the pillows, to the hard bench and even into the earth beneath it. The tears had stopped, but their dry tracks still scored his cheeks. Slowly, he moved his head from side to side. Then a few words flowed from his mouth, into the darkness, "Why? How could this have happened? This has to be the darkest day of my life. How could things have gone so badly, so quickly? Those people today, they weren't people. They were a mob. They might have killed me. Why? I didn't do anything wrong! I don't deserve this! It isn't fair!" And on it went, into the darkness.

As long as he could remember, Daedalus was content to fill his days with work. So much of himself was willingly poured into this working life, day after day. It was what he did. He built many things in this city. How could the citizens reject him like that? Why couldn't his life just keep going on that way, the way it always had? An architect and a builder, that was who he was.

It was all slipping away with this relentless run of bad fortune. There was no balance anymore. He was disoriented. He was suffering.

Like the wall of the courtyard surrounding his house, he wanted to build another one, this one around his heart; a good strong wall, strong enough to guard it forever, or as long as he needed. Silently, he glanced around the room with hollow eyes, making sure, once again, that he was alone inside this private sanctuary.

His entire body was weary. The bruise on his shoulder ached. He remembered the fear, the panic and the anger. The strength of the day's emotions lingered like residue inside of him, dull sensations that would not be easily forgotten. His eyes closed but the memories would not let him sleep.

The embers of the fire grew dimmer still. Daedalus did not notice. His eyes remained shut, head in his hands. It was as if he had blinders on, not wanting to see or to feel anything outside of himself. "Just look at what you have been through," he told himself. "Surely that is enough," he thought despairingly.

His thoughts descended a darkening path. But for all the dimming of the embers around him, there was still another part, deep inside, that recoiled from the despair. It was the part that would not give up, that could continue to dare to hope even in the darkness of that night. A transcendent spark, vital and glowing, it held its own against the anger and the fear. The events of that day had taken a toll, tested him, tested that spark, but the light remained and it glowed as if sourced with an energy separate from his own and independent of all that went on around him.

Feeling drawn to its warmth, he focused on the glow. It would not be cut off. He stood at his own crossroads, balancing the fear and the darkness of that day with the radiance of that spark. He drew in a long, slow breath, held and then blew it into the light; then another breath and another. The flame seemed to respond, shinning just a little brighter. With that thought his sense of the despair began to shift and his spirits no longer drifted downward. Even there, in those depths, there was a choice. It didn't matter so much where he was or how low he had been, the only things that really mattered were the choice of direction and taking the next step.

So he took the next step. He moved away from the path of his descent and saying to himself, "Can there be something else for me, maybe some place away from here?"

The question hung in the air. Out of fear he told himself that it wasn't safe to venture outside of the house. Then anger responded, telling him he could go anywhere he pleased, but he actually had no idea where. The competing emotions skirmished for awhile, vying for control.

"Of course, I can go somewhere else, when I'm ready to leave. And then the boy's mother and everyone else will say that it proves my guilt."

"They will say that anyway, no matter what happens."

"How can I leave all this behind?" he thought he himself, thinking of his house and his property.

"If the next angry crowd takes off my head, then the house might as well be gone." It was the voice of courage rising above the fear and the anger.

"This house is just a building. I can walk away, leave it all behind. And I can leave this city!"

They were the words of a choice being made, a decision that the habits and routines of a lifetime wouldn't rule him any longer. It was the sound of room being made for another round of possibilities. He felt lighter, no longer burdened by the weight of the world. Staring into the last remaining embers, he finally got up for more wood and said nothing at all for a time.

With new pieces of kindling, he stoked the fire and in a few moments the embers turned into dancing flames again. Looking into them, a small smile turned up the end of one side of his lips and he said, "If I could go anywhere at all, where would I choose to go? I'm a free man and there is certainly nothing keeping me here."

He paused and looked around the room, wondering where the idea had come from. Leaving the city of his birth had never occurred to him before. "What about the island of King Minos? Many travelers and merchants speak of it. They say that the city is vibrant and the island beautiful, but that they had a terrible earthquake some years ago."

"Why am I still here?" Daedalus said, answering his own question. "If the city was damaged then the king's palace was too, and surely there is a need for an architect and a builder. It's not far, just a few days sail by boat. There are always boats in the harbor. There may be one getting ready to leave right now."

"Is that good, or is that good!" he teased himself. "The king of that island will not care about my troubles here in Athens. He will care about having the palace rebuilt." On his feet now, Daedalus paced back and forth across the room, feeling the warmth of the light and heat from the fire.

"Why is it so dark in here?" he asked himself, excited now and more than ready to begin. From somewhere, his confidence returned. He felt reassured. He had a goal and that felt good. What he wanted now was a plan. "First things first," he said to himself. "There might even be a ship bound for the island in the harbor right now."

And with that thought, Daedalus left the dark night of his soul behind. He opened the door to his home and walked out into what was left of the darkness, bound for the harbor. He wanted to walk along the shore and look at the ships, see how many there were and learn where they were headed. He walked purposefully again, the way he used to walk when he had something in mind. And as he moved along in the direction of the harbor, he began to think about what he should take with him on the sea voyage and what he would need to start over in a new place. It would mean leaving behind a lot.

"Of course I will need my tools."

"But why? Surely there are tools on the island."

"Money, that is the real tool. Gold. That's really all I need. With gold I can make or buy whatever I want. And I have some, more than enough I'm sure. I worked long and hard for what I have and I've saved a lot, too. I just haven't taken the time to spend it, at least until now."

As he walked along, he made a list in his head of things that he wanted to take with him on the journey, then another list of the things he wanted to do or finish before he left. He was excited and as his planning unfolded, Daedalus arrived at the harbor. There were a handful of ships dotting the sparkling moonlit water. He smiled to himself and wondered which one would carry him and his new dreams away.

Daedalus sat down under a tree, still looking out at the ships on the water in the silence of the night. He imagined himself on one of them sailing across the Aegean and Mediterranean Seas, something he had never done before. He closed his eyes and began to dream. In the dream, he carried two heavy bags. One bag, of course, was full of tools and the other full of some personal things, food and his gold. The bags were never far from his eyes. He imagined the captain and the crew watching him. He observed in the dream, the way that they watched him, as he watched his bags. Surely they would figure out that he was departing Athens for the last time, traveling alone and taking as many of his valuables as he could carry.

Daedalus' heart sank again. He placed his head in his hands and wept, knowing that if he tried so travel to Crete as a wealthy builder, he would surely become fish food. The fatigue and the weariness that had gripped him a few hours before, quickly returned.

So the vigil continued. He sat under a tree in the moonlight. But his eyes no longer watched the ships gently rock upon the sparkling water. They were turned inward again and all he could see was the weariness and the shadows.

Chapter 6

The Threshold

We have to be prepared for change...
~Paulo Coelho, The Alchemist

A young boy stood nearby in the shadows. He watched the brooding man and tried to determine if the man might be drunk or dangerous. He could not see the man's eyes or even his face. It was hidden by his hands. But if he could have seen them, he would have noticed that they were shut tight, only wanting or able to see inward. The man was oblivious to anyone watching him. His head was down and he let out an occasional sigh, as if holding the weight of the world had become too much for him. This man would not be a threat to him, the boy intuited.

The unexpected and dramatic turn of events in his life had completely overwhelmed Daedalus. He didn't want to be faced with any more decisions, not right now. Once he had known how to do it, how to adapt to change, even to find ways to thrive in the face of it. But he was so badly out of practice now. He had been coasting on habits and routines for so long that his skills for learning new things had atrophied from neglect. Even now he was busy telling himself that he couldn't cope with any more change in his life, that he didn't want to have to see or hear anything new or unexpected and that would no doubt have included the movement of approaching feet, young ones, coming closer and closer.

The boy was probably about eight years old, but he wasn't exactly sure. No one had been around to keep track of his birthdays for a long time. Age just wasn't that important to him, not in the same way that speed, a quick wit and agility were. That's what served the boy when it came to finding his next meal without getting hurt in the process. Those traits and a few others were the ones that he cultivated.

He had been watching the man for a while, long enough to know that he was still alive and that he didn't smell or act like a drunken man. The movement in the shoulders and the occasional sob told him that much. The boy moved closer, step by step to the much larger man. The boy kept his courage in sight and kept moving, all the time poised and ready to jump back and flee at the first sign of danger.

Experience had taught him that artful begging would be the best approach with this one, if he could get his attention and the young boy moved in upon the large, sulking target. When he was close enough but still out of arms reach, he extended one arm and lifted his hand palm upward. He stood there a moment in silence, hoping for the right words to come and then just as he opened his mouth to speak, the man stirred. Daedalus must have heard or felt the approach. He returned to the present moment with a jolt that surprised both of them.

He turned in the direction of the approaching sound and stared hard at the intruder. The boy stayed right there, resisting the sudden urge to flee, his open hand still outstretched. He did not move or speak. Instead Daedalus relaxed his face into a smile and spoke first, asking, "Who are you? What are you doing out here in the middle of the night?"

The boy just shrugged, careful to stay out of reach. Then, looking up, he asked for money and food. The words were spoken without affect or emotion, the boy looked up to see how the man responded. It had not begun the way he expected and that made him nervous. Usually, he was the one who had to speak first to an adult in order to get their attention, or to even be noticed.

A few days before, Daedalus probably would not have noticed, either. This night was different, to be sure. Daedalus was still reeling from his encounter with the angry crowd a few days before. All of them against him and some of them expressing it with rocks and sticks. The memory of it stung him deeply. But one of its consequences was that tonight he had no other business to attend to, no other place to be.

In this most unusual time and place, he had the time and the presence to want to have a conversation with a skinny, emotionless boy. He looked first at the boy's face and then up and down the skinny body, eyeing the ragged clothes. He tried to meet the boy's eyes, feeling compassion for this youth who had appeared out of nowhere; someone who, by all appearances, knew very well the sting of rejection.

Daedalus smiled at him again, not wanting him to leave. Softly he asked, "When did you last eat?"

The downcast eyes looked away and again the boy shrugged. He said nothing, but the hand remained outstretched.

Daedalus didn't give up. He looked at him quizzically and asked, "Where's your mother? Your father?"

Another shrug in reply.

Daedalus smiled at the boy and spoke again, "I have no food here, but we can have breakfast at my home. It's over there, near that large rock by the central part of the city. There's food there and you can have as much as you want."

Daedalus motioned for the boy to come closer, but the boy just stood there, warily keeping his distance, watching. The hand was still outstretched. So Daedalus reached into his pocket and pulled out a handful of coins. He reached over toward the boy and with his closed hand slightly above the boy's palm began emptying the handful of coins from his large hand into the smaller outstretched one. The boy's other hand quickly rose and joined the pursuit, moving quick as a flash to catch each one in the air, breaking into a slight smile with the accomplishment. That look of satisfaction was the only hint of emotion that the boy showed to the man, but he did look up into Daedalus' eyes and thanked him.

Daedalus Rising

"Come and walk with me and there will be more for you when we get to my home." Daedalus said and with that he stood up, turned and began walking away. The boy did not follow and Daedalus walked on for a few steps without stopping or turning around.

Not until the boy called out, "What do you want for the money?"

Daedalus turned and smiled at the boy, catching his eyes this time and replied, "The money is yours to keep. You can have it all and just walk away if that is your wish. But if you want to have breakfast, then come with me to my house. It's up to you."

There was a pause, neither one knowing quite what to do next. They looked at each other momentarily, each one considering the choices. The kernel of an idea had begun to form in the mind of the builder and he broke the silence, asking the boy, "Are you happy here in Athens?"

Without hesitation, "When I have food!"

Daedalus smiled and renewed the invitation, "Then let's go eat some," and he turned and started away again.

With those words, the boy began to follow and Daedalus retraced his steps back through the empty streets of Athens, heading home one more time. The boy stayed a few steps behind, always out of arms reach. They walked for a long time like that, mostly in silence, the sky grew lighter with the sun's approach. As they walked, Daedalus kept to his own thoughts. His idea had grown and now it took hold of him, fanning the flame of hope that he had encountered the night before. It caused the flame to flare just a little brighter. Finally, they neared the wall of the courtyard that surrounded his home. Daedalus gave the idea voice, turned around and asked the boy, "What is your name son?"

"Icarus," the boy replied. "My name is Icarus."

Now Daedalus stopped. He turned and bent down on one knee so that they were about the same height and he looked directly into the boy's face. Calmly, evenly and smiling at the boy and he said, "Icarus. I have to leave on a journey soon and I am inviting you to come along. If you decide to come on this journey, then I promise that I will keep you safe and see that you are never hungry."

Icarus didn't say anything at first and Daedalus didn't wait for an answer. Instead, he stood back up, opened the door to the courtyard and walked inside. Icarus followed. Once inside the house Daedalus headed straight for the kitchen, where he prepared a huge breakfast for the two of them, telling stories and laughing the entire time. It was quite a contrast from the somber tones of the nights before.

They ate heartily and while they ate, Daedalus told Icarus of his plans to travel to a distant island, right away and that they had to sail on a ship to get there. He told Icarus of his plan to travel as a blind man, with a young boy as his guide. A blind man with just enough money to pay for the voyage and not much more. With the plan laid out, Daedalus winked at Icarus and asked, "Can you be my guide?"

Without so much as a moment's hesitation, Icarus smiled back and said, "When do we leave?"

Icarus ate a huge amount of food and when he was through, went outside to explore the courtyard. He fell asleep in the warm morning sunlight and Daedalus began making his plans. One unobtrusive bag would be enough, filled with dried food for two, a few necessities and one favorite tool, his level.

The bag nearly packed, Daedalus began making his decisions about the money, just the right amount of it. The amount that a poor blind man would be expected to take on a voyage such as this, an amount that would not attract attention. He decided it was ten coins of gold and that much he would carry openly in a small bag.

He planned to wear a heavy tunic on the voyage. It was a stout garment, perfect for travel. Picking it up in one hand, he held it by the collar and then with the other, cut the seams with a sharp knife. Then he sewed gold coins into the fabric. Not so many that he wouldn't be able to move around comfortably on the ship, but enough with which to make a new start on the island.

Daedalus Rising

Later that day, a blind man and a young Icarus returned to the harbor. They found the captain of a ship leaving for the island and were able to agree on a price for passage for the two of them. They learned that the journey might only take four days with fair wind and to be ready to depart at first light.

For his part, the captain learned that the blind man had more money than sense, having willingly paid three times the amount that his last passenger had. Without saying the words, Daedalus had shown himself to be a man in a hurry to leave and now the captain wondered what other secrets the blind man and the boy had.

Early the next morning, Daedalus and Icarus returned to the harbor, to a sailing ship carrying a red flag with a black silhouette in the center. It was the darkened outline of the horns of a bull. Between them they carried their one bag and in it, all that they would take with them into their new lives on the island.

Boarding the ship, they stepped into their new roles. It was like crossing a threshold or entering a passage way to a different country and a new culture. Icarus played the part of a blind man's guide. Daedalus had his own roles. First was the role of the blind man. Second was that of a man who knew how to watch over and provide for a young boy. There could be no turning back now. It was the start of their journey together and once at sea, there was only one direction, whatever lay ahead.

Chapter 7

The Voyage

> *To live into the future is to leap into the unknown. There are no well-worn paths in this forest, no guides. To live into the future is to trust in the abundance of the universe and that takes courage.*
> ~Rollo May, The Courage to Create

In a distant time, long before the old stories were told to Daedalus by his father, ships were driven about by the labor of many strong backs pulling at long oars. Navigation was neither an art nor much of an issue, because in those times ships did not travel out of sight of land. Instead they journeyed from one place to the next following the coastline. Travel by any means was slow and few people engaged in it.

Since then huge technological advances had taken place. Ships were fitted with a single large sail, rigged to horizontal spar on a mast that rose out of the ship's midsection. With a sail to catch the wind, large ships could now skim across the water carrying just a small crew instead of many and moving from one place to the next as directly as the wind would allow. With these advances came the idea of voyaging along a direct line, charting a course out across the water to arrive at a destination, foregoing the surety of following the coast line and the time that it entailed. Places that had once been unreachable became destinations, as long as there was enough fortitude to make the journey. It was a matter of finding the right combination of courage, reckless innocence and simple faith to sail out into an endless sea beyond the sight of land, with only the stars, a compass and whatever food and water you could carry.

Before this voyage, neither Daedalus nor Icarus had ever been away from Athens. For each in his own way, boarding the ship for the first time was very much like the experience of those early mariners. Stepping aboard that morning was a leap into the unknown, letting go so that they could be swept into the currents of their journey and wherever it would take them.

As the passengers came aboard, the crew was busy unfurling and setting the large sail. A large leaping fish was painted in the center, a cerulean compliment to the hues of the sky and the sea. Icarus laughed and explained the painted sail to Daedalus, falling into his new role right from the start. One of the crew soon joined in, telling them that the large fish was called a porpoise and how useful it was for guiding the ship across the water. The five person crew hauled in the anchor as the sun came up and slowly they pulled away from the harbor, leaving the city of Athens behind and heading south. The captain and the crew were going home. A light, favorable wind came up, pushing them across the water and it was exciting to feel the ship pick up speed. Right up until that point, either one of them might have been able to change his mind and return to shore, but no longer. They were underway and whatever fears they had brought along began to slip away, just like the land steadily receded from view.

Of course, Daedalus did not let on that he could actually see what was happening, especially that points of land were no longer visible. Instead, he tried to make a point of not noticing these things. He was in his role, acting the proper blind man, just as Icarus was in his, happily chatting about everything that was going on around them. He was excited and full of energy. The journey had begun.

If there was any sadness or regret, any fear or anxiety, Icarus certainly didn't show it, not once they set sail and started moving. Daedalus asked, more than once, how he felt to be leaving Athens, maybe for the last time. Without any hesitation at all, Icarus replied that as long as he could remember, he had wanted to travel to places far away. He had even gone to the harbor the night that they met, because he liked to look at the ships and to dream about sailing away on one. It seemed to Icarus that meeting that night had been an omen, a good one and everything that had happened since was in accord with his dream and his purpose. He felt truly happy about the way events unfolded and it was an exciting time for him. Icarus reassured him that he was more than ready to leave Athens and left nothing behind. He did not remember anyone but his mother ever taking care of him and she had been gone for so long.

Daedalus on the other hand, was leaving quite a lot behind. He was full of regrets and sadness about the way things could have been or should have been and throughout the voyage, he would often turn these thoughts over in his mind, reexamining his choices and wondering if it could ever be worth all the cost and the effort.

Not surprisingly, for Daedalus the days at sea were long and slow, filled with bright sun, salt air and time. Sometimes to break the tedium, he would shuffle around the deck with Icarus as his guide. Of course, it was not so large a boat and no matter how slow his gait, a circuit did not take very long. Other times, the sighting of a fish or a turtle, sometimes even a porpoise, would break the tedium. Often Daedalus reminded himself to ask Icarus to describe some of it for him and it didn't take long before Icarus began to invent some very new and unusual fish to entertain them both. Sometimes a crew member listened in, joining in the amusement.

It was different for Icarus. Each day was its own adventure and he seemed to have no trouble at all occupying his time with interesting things to do. There was the bucket made of animal hide, used by the crew to bring cool water up from the sea and onto the deck. Pouring cool water over his head on a hot day was a dependable source of pleasure and relief and fun too, when he poured some unexpectedly over the head of a man who was pretending to be blind.

Daedalus Rising

After a few days at sea, Daedalus began to notice how much enjoyment he took in trying to keep up with Icarus and his tricks, especially through a long, hot afternoon. It did not take long at all for him to figure out how much he enjoyed just having the young boy around for company.

Mostly the captain ignored them, treating them more like cargo and that was the habit of the crew as well. No one seemed to care very much about what they did as long as they stayed out of the way. Of all of the crew, it was the captain who seemed to make a point of being distant and aloof. But, undaunted by his ambivalence, each day Icarus would find an excuse to approach him and ask, "How much longer, sir?"

Each day the Captain would just return a blank stare, stroke at his beard once or twice as if considering whether to answer at all and then summon up the same monotone reply, "Pray for fair wind, boy."

The True Story of Icarus

Chapter 8

The Gatekeeper

> *If you do not express your own original ideas, if you do not listen to your own being, you will have betrayed yourself. Also you will have betrayed your community in failing to make your contribution to the whole.*
> ~Rollo May, The Courage to Create

With the dawn of the fourth day, land was in sight. It was a distant massive expanse of dull green and brown, shrouded by clouds and rising right up out of the sea. A mountain top in purple and green capped the island, peeking out through the clouds. After four days at sea, it was all a welcome sight. Still many miles from shore the island took up the entire horizon as far as they could see. If this was their destination, then it was a huge island. While Icarus described the landscape, the friendliest of the sailors assured them that they had indeed arrived. With some pride, he explained that the mountain was named Mount Ida and that melting snow from its snowcapped peak provided much of the fresh water for the city that lay below. According to the Greek myths this mountain was the birthplace of Zeus, the king of the gods, making it convenient for the island's ruler, King Minos, the lawgiver, to receive his guidance locally.

They sailed all day, running to the southwest and gradually closing the distance to the shore. They all shared a common desire for the voyage to be over and as the afternoon wore on, it became more and more apparent. Caught up in his own eagerness Daedalus began to consider the many things he wanted to do when they reached the land. He decided that it was time to talk with the captain and learn about the best ways for strangers to find food and shelter in a new city.

Ahead of them, the sun set into a picturesque orange and red sky. The ship rounded a sharp point of land revealing a large natural bay. As the bay unfolded a small settlement of white and grey buildings perched on the waters edge, came into view. The two travelers, eager to be off the ship and heartened by the sight, both began to talk and laugh and to point toward the shoreline. The captain and crew enjoyed the view as well, but they couldn't help but notice the blind man pointing to the shore as he talked to the young boy. The captain watched a moment longer, then he quietly walked to the helmsman and instructed him to bring the boat about and head back out to sea.

As the boat came around, the passengers turned the other way, wanting to keep the harbor in sight. An abrupt change in course so close to the land, something was wrong. Now Daedalus really had a reason to talk to the captain, right away and he asked Icarus to lead the way. Daedalus tried to get his attention, but the captain kept himself busy talking with the crew. He brushed Daedalus away with a wave of his hand, curtly saying that just then, there was no time for talk.

A few moments before, the deck had been a joyful place. Now there was an air of foreboding. Through the cool evening air, they sailed on into the growing twilight. In the first moments after the ship turned, Icarus was certain that something had gone very wrong. It was the sense of hope leaving and he considered jumping over the side and swimming for it. But he was not a swimmer. He would only have been trying to swim and there was no hope that way either. So he rode through the turn and watched the land recede, hands clenched to the rail, as the sinking feeling in his stomach grew.

After putting a few more miles between the ship and the harbor, the captain ordered the sail gathered in. The crew responded in silence and without hesitation. The ship quickly stalled, losing momentum and drifting upon the water. Icarus tried to keep the island in view through the gathering darkness.

The True Story of Icarus

It was barely visible now, a hazy blur on the horizon. With the sail secured, it became so quiet that Daedalus could hear the waves gently lapping on the wooden hull. The sound seemed to reach to him through a daze. He remembered a dream he had once had, long ago, something about a gift.

The crew stood about the deck, attentive, as if waiting for something to happen. Icarus felt it too. Even since turning away from the island, the tension mounted on the deck. Now it seemed about to overflow. Why wasn't Daedalus doing something? Icarus felt his own fear but kept his silence, not wanting to draw attention to himself. There was nowhere to go but he pushed his back down against the rail as low as he could, making himself as small and unobtrusive as he could possibly be.

The captain, who had said so little during the voyage, broke the silence. It was a deep, resonate voice, one that he saved for those rare times when he really wanted a sailor's attention. He had never used it on Daedalus or Icarus, not during the voyage. Not until he said, "Blind man! Come over here. Follow the sound of my voice. And you, boy, stay by the rail. Let him find his own way."

What else could Daedalus do, but obey? "Don't worry," was all he said.

Then he began his slow blind man's shuffle across the deck and over to where the captain stood. As he approached, a crew member stepped in behind him. Two more silently approached him from the front. Each held one end of a long spar, just above the level of the deck, ahead of his ankles. Daedalus, of course, could see everything that was happening. They made him choose between responding to the approaching nemesis as a sighted man, or instead to continue his silent groping shuffle. Neither option seemed to hold a great deal of promise so he stayed in his role as a blind man, playing out the hand he had dealt himself.

Two open hands struck the middle of his back, roughly shoving him ahead. His feet rushed forward to catch his weight,

Daedalus Rising

but the ankles collided with the spar and Daedalus toppled forward, crashing to the wooden deck. Before he could get out of the way, the two sailors brought the long pole up and over his back, bringing it down hard against the nape of his neck, pushing his face against the wooden beams of the deck. He groaned involuntarily as his face scraped across the deck and brought his hands under his shoulders to push back against the downward force of the spar. He groaned again, deeper this time, as a well placed foot hit him in the ribs, telling him it was not a good time for resistance. The sailors on each end of the spar pushed down harder still and Daedalus lay pinned to the deck unable to move, his arms and legs still. He could only see the one man, far out of reach and with a secure hold on his end of the pole. Unable to see anyone else, he could hear them moving, coming closer and he feared the next blow.

Icarus didn't say a word. Terrified, he hardly breathed. Running at the first sign of danger had been a particular specialty of his. In Athens, he had learned very early to avoid the situation that he couldn't run away from. It was the law of the jackrabbit and he knew it well. At the first sign of danger, he was gone. But here on this ship, there was no escape, nowhere to run. All he could do was make himself as small as possible. He stared at the men on the deck, stealthily moving along the rail, backing away from all of them.

The captain walked over to where Daedalus lay sprawled upon the deck. He stood next to the prone man for a few seconds without speaking, displaying neither concern nor urgency. Then in the same voice, he said "Do not get up off the deck of my ship."

Daedalus did not move. He did not speak.

"Blind man," the captain continued, "let me tell you a story, the story of a rich man who had to flee from Athens in peril for his life. It's an interesting story. This man, he left in a hurry on a ship bound for an island ruled by King Minos, disguised as a poor blind man and led about by a young boy. You must have heard it. It was the talk of the harbor back in Athens. But I can't

The True Story of Icarus

seem to remember the name. What was that man's name? Tell me Athenian, what did he do that he had to leave so quickly?"

Daedalus didn't respond. Icarus had moved into his field of vision and Daedalus watched him, hunched over, pushing against the rail. He saw a very scared boy and even through his own discomfort, Daedalus felt badly that he had brought him to this end.

Following Daedalus' gaze, the Captain turned and looked over to the frightened Icarus, saying: "Icarus, we are still very far from land, too far away for even a swimmer like you to make it to shore. You had best stay on board a while longer." Then he turned back to Daedalus and cast him a malevolent grin, taunting him and asking, "Aren't you curious to know what happens next?"

The words cut away whatever shreds of hope Daedalus harbored. He felt as helpless as a beached whale, immobilized and bloated, full of fear and frustration. "This is not good at all." he thought to himself. "What can I do? I have to say something." He remembered the gold in his bag and felt a little of his own composure returning. Mustering as much determination as he could, he said, "We have gold in our bag. Take it. It is yours. But keep your word! Take us into shore." Wanting to sound determined, he forced out the words, garbled by the pressure of his face against the wooden deck. As he spoke, he could feel the weight of the spar on the back of his neck lessen a little, as if the sailors had heard his words clearly enough. That was a good sign too.

"You, the one who is not so blind after all. What would you teach me of promises and truth telling?" responded the captain.

"You promised to take us to the island!'

"I promised to take a blind man," the captain shouted back. "And that is what I did. We were there just this afternoon. Right before you showed us that you are nothing but a smuggler with normal sight. It is only the smuggler that did not reach the island. As for the gold, you are correct. It belongs to me and the crew now. Including the gold coins sewn into your tunic, the

Daedalus Rising

ones that are clanking onto the deck of this ship. It is a tax upon your lies! Take off that robe."

Laying face down, the pole held tight against his neck, Daedalus could not begin to move enough to comply with the demand. All he could do was make a few futile twists of his arms. He was already tired from the ordeal and there was no point in wasting what was left of his energy. So he lay still and waited.

The captain would not wait. A knife appeared in his right hand and he reached down with his left, grabbing the collar of the tunic. With one strong pull he jerked upward on the garment. The right hand made a smooth arc across the prone man's back. Icarus caught his breath. The knife sliced neatly across the garment as the left hand pulled upwards, freeing it from the shoulders. It tore up and away from Daedalus' back. As the garment rose upwards in a sweeping arc, gold coins began spewing out of the lining as if it were a fountain. Even in the semi-darkness, they gleamed as they flew through the air, each one in its own separate arc. Everyone on the deck was fixated at the sight of the coins sailing through the air. Even the two sailors who held fast the opposite ends of the spar dropped their holds, distracted by the gleaming metal. One by one the coins rained down onto the deck and thudded onto the wood, some of them rolling away and others spun about like tops on an axis. The entire crew scrambled, lunged and grabbed for the coins, knocking into anything and anyone that was in the way.

Daedalus was freed from the entrapment of the pole, only to be caught in the center of the melee. Knees and elbows struck him in the head and back as several sailors threw themselves across him as they dove for rolling coins. The quickest hands won and in a few seconds, it was over. The coins had new homes in the pockets of different tunics, but at least, he was no longer pinned to the deck. That much was a good thing. Daedalus looked around to see the captain unmoved, standing nearby and watching him. He still had the knife in his hand. Wearily, he watched another sailor carrying his bag out onto the deck. Daedalus watched as his bag was turned upside down and what was left of their belongings spilled out: his level, some cloths, their rations of dried fruit and a small locked box which the captain quickly took for his own.

Tears came to Daedalus' eyes as he slumped to the deck, this time of his own accord. He felt empty and exhausted from the trials of being caught in his own intrigue. They had stripped it all away from him. Everything was gone, everything. He once thought that he was so clever. And all those years of toil back in Athens, for what? He had left so much behind and now the rest was gone as well. Hadn't he lost enough? He just wanted a little security. Was that asking so much? He had worked long and hard for his money. He had a right to try and keep it, didn't he? Now it was gone. He was certain that there was no justice, anywhere. Defeat and emptiness washed over him.

Icarus watched from the rail of the ship. He could see defeat on the shirtless man, lying on the deck. "Not me," Icarus declared to himself. "I'm not giving in. If they try to come after me, I can take my chances in the water." He was sure that he could swim a little. Maybe there was a log floating out on the water. Or maybe another boat would come along and pick him up. He was not about to give up.

Daedalus, on the other hand, felt as if he had fallen from a great height and had the wind was knocked out of him. A man of wealth and position in Athens, he had devolved into a broken man lying on the deck of a pirate ship. "Everything that I ever had is gone," he thought. "Taken away, stolen, right before my eyes and there was nothing I could do to stop it." With that thought, he looked up and saw a small boy, staring at him from the rail. The boy shook and he looked scared. But he also kept rising up and looking over the side, as if he was going to jump for it. Daedalus was scared too, very scared. He wondered again for at least the hundredth time, why he ever wanted to leave Athens. Once more time he blamed the mother of the boy that fell off the roof. He blamed the politician for stirring up the community. He even tried to find a way to blame the boy that

Daedalus Rising

died. He blamed everyone he could think of blaming, but as he looked over at Icarus about to throw himself into the dark water, he said quietly to himself, "And none of that matters a bit. The only thing here of any importance, is his life and mine."

His compassion for Icarus' plight resonated with his own desire to live, to keep going. From somewhere, he understood that he still had something to offer, something of value and importance. His captors could never take away from him. Surely it would be enough.

Daedalus sat up, looked toward the captain and said in a calm but resolute voice, "I have your answer."

Everyone on the ship turned and looked directly him.

"The name of the builder that fled from Athens in such a hurry, his name is Daedalus. And I am that man. I was once the architect and builder for the king of Athens and Icarus and I have come to your island because your king needs our help to rebuild his palace. He will know of my deeds and reputation."

As he spoke the words his confidence began to return. His words grew in power as he gazed at the captain, catching his eyes with his own and saying "And the king will reward you, when you take us to him."

The captain and the crewmembers quickly glanced around the deck. Each looked to the others, nodding their silent agreement that a reward would be a fine thing. In that moment, in some universal unspoken language, it was agreed to spare his life.

The captain spoke next, giving the order to set the sail and make for land once again. Catching the breeze the ship slowly came about. Daedalus stood up and felt the cool wind against his back. It was over. He was free of having his face pressed into the deck and free of his self-imposed masquerade. He was Daedalus - the architect - once again.

Icarus saw it all from his vantage point just beneath the rail of the ship. His breathing was back to normal, but he wasn't ready to come out and show himself. He would stay as small as he could for a while longer.

The captain and crew returned to their usual duties, as if nothing out of the ordinary had happened. Not so easy for Daedalus. Slowly he made his way over to where Icarus hid. As the man came nearer, Icarus spoke out as if challenging him and asking, "So what happens when we get to the island? Is that king really going to hire you to rebuild his palace? I need to know, because I can make other plans."

"Yes," said Daedalus. "All that and more will happen once we arrive on the island. The king has a great need for someone like me and this island can be our new home. I feel like I have just been given the chance to make a new life here. Icarus, after tonight, you have a part to play in all that. You are young and your whole life is ahead of you. On this island, you'll have the chance to make your life anyway you can imagine it. And I will have the same chance, even if I am a little older."

Icarus didn't say anything, but he listened to the words.

"I know that your instincts tell you that as soon as the ship gets close enough to land, to run away as fast and as far as you can. But listen to me. The danger is gone and there is no need to run anymore. More than that, I intend to keep the promise I made in Athens. After this experience tonight, I could never lie to you or to anyone else. And I am promising you that I will keep you safe and see that you are never hungry, just as your father would."

He and Icarus sat together on the deck and talked for a long time about the voyage, about what had happened that day and what they wanted to do when they finally got to the harbor. It was good for them to talk, because they had each faced many fears that night. Somehow Daedalus found the right words to reach out and soothe the darker ones that had come up for Icarus, a boy who had long since given up on the idea of trust. Now, Daedalus told him that he was different; that he was someone who could be trusted and that they were even going to have a home in this new place.

"Well," thought Icarus to himself, "I'll believe it when it happens."

Daedalus Rising

Later that night, the ship made it back to the harbor and the anchor was set. They were so close to land that Icarus could smell it, the salt and sweat of the harbor, blending with the earthy fragrance of the trees and the land. In the morning, the people would come out of their houses. Now they were close enough, for sure. He could swim and run and quickly lose himself in the dark shadows of the buildings on the land. But he didn't. He chose instead to stay on board with Daedalus, wanting to see what the next day would bring.

Chapter 9

The Dreamtime

*I rise ecstatic through all and sweep with the true gravitation,
the whirling and whirling is elemental within me.*
~Walt Whitman, Leaves of Grass

Daedalus stood and leaned his weight against the rail of the ship. He looked out across the water to the sleeping village on the other side of the bay. Tired and dazed, he stood without moving for a long time, watching a silver sliver of a moon rise higher and higher into the sky. Not far away, Icarus was sound asleep, curled up on a sleeping hide. Sleep would not come for the man. So much had happened that night; the energies of fear and anger were replaced with a willing neutrality within him. From time to time, he paced back and forth across the deck. He tried to distract himself by looking ahead and imagining what the palace was like and the city that surrounded it. It was still miles away overland, in the foothills of the mountains. Soon, he thought it would be his home. He held onto that idea for awhile and then expanded it to include Icarus and that both of them would have the home.

He smiled at the shift in perspective. The events of the evening worked some changes. From deep in the depths of his own fear a few hours before, now he was feeling gracious. Icarus had gone there with him. He never expected anything like that to happen, not to either one of them and he regretted Icarus' unintended involvement. But they had both come through it and all in all, he was glad that the boy was there. Now that it was over and they were finally at the island, it surprised him to realize how much he wanted Icarus to trust him.

"He is so young and vulnerable," Daedalus thought, making the inevitable comparison, "much younger than the other boy back in Athens." At least that boy had a family that cared about him. Icarus has no one else; no one but me." He recalled their last conversation and the commitment that he just renewed.

With those thoughts and many others filling his head, an exhausted Daedalus gathered his sleeping hide and laid it out near the boy. Then he lay back onto the wooden beams of the deck, propped the empty traveling bag beneath his head and stared up at the stars, just as he had done every night since they left Athens. He lay back and felt the enveloping power and presence of the night sky.

After a time, his eyes did close and he began to sleep, a deep, restful sleep. In the dream that followed, he found himself standing barefoot on a large green, rectangular field, bordered by hills and tall trees. He was all alone in the middle of a bright blue cloudless day with the sun directly overhead. In the center of the field, there was a prominent mound, covered over with soft grasses. He walked towards it.

Instead of going straight to the top, he circled around the flank, moving in an ascending spiral and aware of a breeze that began to blow. At the top, he rotated his bearded face into that steady breeze, feeling the force on his torso, legs and hands. His skin tingled with the warmth and glow of the sunlight mixing it's potency with the wind. The tingling sensations became a shiver that spread from his chest and arms, down into the legs and even into his toes. The vibration passed through his feet and into the ground. The earth answered back. A sudden pulse of bright vitality stung the bottoms of his feet in the grass. A wave of energy surged up his legs and into his body. The right knee moved and rotated outward, drawn upward into the focus of the sun's light. The shoulders twisted, following the knee's rotation. His body followed. The right arm rose, pulled by the same attraction and the left quickly followed. With each arm extended, the shoulders followed and he began to spin. Palms open, the wrists twisted them toward the sunlight. Effortlessly, his body was drawn in an upward spiral into the light and warmth of the sun. Stretched out to its full length, only the left foot remained in contact with the grassy earth. And then, one by one, his toes lifted off, freeing him to embrace the sky, trusting in a ride that became more magnificent with each second.

Moving upward in an ever expanding spiral, he felt relaxed and at peace, right until the moment when he looked down and tried to find the hill where he stood just a few moments before. It was already blurred into the broader expanse of the field and he tensed up, taking his eyes away from the ground. Anxiety was creeping in with the increasing elevation, but he continued in the upward spiral, moving away from the field that was now a small rectangle in the midst of rolling green woodlands. Beyond them the rolling hills gave way to rocky cliffs and beaches; all of it rose up out of a beautiful sea.

His upward path expanded outward until eventually it reached a point where the gravitational attraction through the sun diminished and his chest was no longer pulled by its irresistible attraction. Instead, he could feel the opposing force of the earth's gravity, directing him back. Giving into the adverse forces he extended his arms fully and banked away from his ascent. Almost at once, he began to lose altitude, not free falling exactly, but in an awkward glide that moved his body through a slow descending arc. It was a measured decline, a delicate balance between fields of opposing gravitational flux and it was glorious. Just like flying! Or was it floating? He wasn't sure what to call it. But whatever it was, there was never anything like it before.

Then quite by accident he slid into an equilibrium, a precise but invisible place where the two gravities cancelled one another exactly. For just that moment, he was stable and balanced in the sky and he believed that he might now know how it felt to soar like an eagle or an albatross; something large and with a great wingspan, enough to hold his own body aloft and to ride upon the winds.

Daedalus Rising

So much excitement packed into a single delicious dream and the pleasure of it went on and on, until he found himself wondering how and where he would eventually land. Looking out across the island, he considered whether he had the elevation to glide out in a controlled descent past the shoreline and to end the flight in the sea. Surely that was the best option. And with thoughts of landing in his head, the dream began to unwind. He tried to twist and rotate into the upward flow, but could not find it again. Instead, he steadily lost altitude, descending through the currents in the air, as his momentum took him constantly downward along a broad arc, back towards the field where he began.

The shift had taken place so quickly, in just the blink of an eye. There was no time to turn and head out to sea; there was not enough elevation, no room left in the sky. He had to make do with the soft earth of the grassy field. The upward lift from the sun's gravity faded rapidly and without it, there was only what remained of the momentum of his glide against a steady and rapid decline into a very solid earth, rising up fast to greet him. Even so, the grassy field had to be better than the trees. And there it was in his line of sight, coming up fast. He could see the individual treetops passing by underneath. Watching this he readily saw how fast he was moving; much too fast to catch another uplift, even if one could be found. And as trees opened up to the green field beneath him he thought about the eagles again, knowing that each of them had to have a first landing. He just had to get through the first one. There was no right or wrong to it. It was simply a matter of finishing what he had started.

Just before the collision, he dropped his arms to cradle his head and rolled over onto one side, shielding himself as best he could. His body slid along the ground in a kind of horizontal collision with the grass and soft dirt and sand of the green field. The earth separated into a dark furrow which enveloped his body, grasping him firmly in its embrace. In this way, his forward momentum was finally spent and his body halted, half in and

The True Story of Icarus

half out of the earth. He was still breathing. Daedalus stood up and looked around, wanting to look back across the field and examine the point of contact, but the sand and dirt were everywhere. Brushing it away from his head and face, he blinked his eyes open.

The green field was gone. The dirt and the grass were all gone. Daedalus was awake, lying on the wooden deck of a ship. The ship was at anchor. He was completely intoxicated with the memory and with the thrill of flight. Every cell of his body tingled in the memory. It was the best, the most exhilarating dream there had ever been or ever could be.

The dawn began to light up the sky beyond the hills to the east of the harbor. It was early and the ship was quiet, but there would be no more sleep for him that night. He was wide awake, full and flooded with the memory of flying over the island. He walked, skipped and danced along the deck of the ship, reveling in the memory of it, reliving the sensations of flight and filling his head with the memories and already hoping for the dream to come again.

Chapter 10

To The Palace

An oyster opens his mouth to swallow one drop.
Now there's a pearl...
Don't be satisfied with poems
and stories of how things have gone for others.
Unfold your own myth,
without complicated explanation,
so everyone will understand the passage.

~Rumi

The ship was anchored in the calm water of the bay about one hundred meters off shore. Directly ahead lay a quiet beach, a small village and a short pier jutting out into the water. Only a few shore birds moved about in the morning mist. In the low lying fog, the pier had the look of a crooking forefinger, beckoning welcome and offering freedom and excitement. Icarus stood on the bow and was caught in the attraction. "It will be so good to be off this ship," he said.

Daedalus smiled at him and nodded, but said nothing in response. His mind was far away, still caught in the presence of the dream. He tilted his head slightly to one side, engrossed in the memory and still mindful of the sense of soaring on the winds. Icarus noticed the motion and expected him to respond, but Daedalus was silent. After his flight dream, the proximity of the land just wasn't that important.

They would be going ashore soon enough. Getting to shore was all Icarus could talk about and he looked up at Daedalus. It

The True Story of Icarus

was clear Daedalus wasn't listening. Icasrus finally asked, "Hey, are you awake yet?"

He might have talked about the dream, but decided against it. So fresh in his memory it was like a rare and precious thing, something to be protected, nurtured. He couldn't confide in any of the sailors, not after last night and Icarus probably wouldn't understand. He would tell the story of the dream when he was ready. This just wasn't the time and as for the real meaning, he wasn't sure of that yet either. He still tried to piece together everything that had happened and to understand whether the dream was part of that context. Was it purely a random event, or was it connected to the struggle on the deck of the ship?

He looked over at Icarus, realizing that the boy had spoken to him, but Icarus turned away now, stared out across the water at the shore birds prancing in the surf.

The dream had made such a positive impact. It was like a release from all the routines and perceptions of his life in Athens. Back in that time and place, he might still be seething with resentment or anger over the theft of his money. But since the dream, he was too full of hope to stay angry. The sea voyage was over, but the journey to the palace was just beginning. Last night, the ship's crew was his foe. In the light of day, they had somehow become his compatriots. The sailors would soon lead them to the palace. Their captain was on his way to schedule an audience with the king for them. The irony of the role reversal made him smile. But it wasn't the roles that had changed at all, only his perception of them. Perhaps that was part of the meaning of the dream.

Icarus stood off by himself and Daedalus turned towards him and asked, "What a difference a day can make, don't you think?"

More than the words that were spoken, Icarus heard the ease in the voice, which he understood as an expression of agreement with his own eagerness to be off the ship. "How much longer do we have to wait?" he responded with a question of his own.

Daedalus Rising

"I'm not sure. I don't know where the palace is or how to get there. All I know is that it is going to happen and soon."

Sensing his good humor, Icarus joined him at the rail and put words to what was in his mind, "I'm going to leap off the ship and skim over the water to the shore." The words came out like an announcement and Daedalus felt both the humor and the impatience that inspired them. The older man thought about leaping into the water to keep up with the fleeing boy, but couldn't get past the image of himself, trying to skim across water and the inevitable sinking and splashing that would follow. The sound of their laughter attracted a curious crewmember, who joined them at the rail.

They both grew quiet at the man's approach, but then Daedalus decided to draw him into the conversation, asking, "What name do you go by?"

"Panos is my name," said the man, flashing a quick smile to each of them.

"So Panos, tell us, how do we get to the palace from here?"

"It's less than a day's walk," Panos replied. "The palace is in the center of the capital city and sits on the side of the mountain beyond those hills." He pointed a thick, muscular forefinger to a spot where the harbor town ended and the green wooded hillside began. "There is a road on the other side of the village that follows the course of the river up into the hills. If you follow that road far enough and avoid the turnoffs that take you away from the course of the river, you will get there."

"What is the city like?" Icarus wanted to know.

"You will like it. Both of you will, I can promise you that," he said, making no effort to downplay his pride. "It's not at all like Athens. It's much better." He winked at Icarus.

"How can it be so different from Athens?" Daedalus pressed him. "They are both cities with lots of people and people are the same wherever you go."

"It's just different here. You will see. Athens looks to me as if it has stood too long in the sun and all the color has bleached away. Everything is in shades of white and grey and brown. In our city, everywhere you look the walls are decorated in the colors and patterns of the earth and the sea. We have a huge public courtyard for ceremonies and speeches and performances with dancers and musicians. I have sailed all over the Mediterranean and Aegean seas and I can tell you, there is no place better to live. You will see." Panos smiled at them reassuringly.

"You must have grown up here," Daedalus responded, "Didn't you have an earthquake a few years ago? Have you rebuilt so quickly?"

"Even after the earthquake, it was still a beautiful city. But you are right. Much of it was shaken to the ground when I was a boy, living on the farm with my family."

"Did you feel the earthquake? What was that like? What happened to you?" Icarus asked, his interest in the conversation growing.

Panos was pleased to continue and he told them his story: He told them that it came in the middle of a dark night. Their farm was just outside the capitol city and he lived there with his parents and brothers and sisters. He and his two brothers were all fast asleep in their bed when a deep rumbling sound woke him up. It was like nothing he had ever heard before. The sound grew louder and louder until it reached the house and actually shook it. The walls, the floors, the ceiling, everything shook. The bed rose up and down by itself, the three brothers held onto each other and cried out as debris dropped onto them from the roof. It was constructed mostly of branches and earth, laid out on a framework between supporting logs. The support beams held. Not so the apartments and buildings in the city, with more than one level. There the floors and roofs were made of wood and stone and there was much damage, especially to the palace. It was much worse there and many people were hurt. Even now they are still rebuilding."

"How often has that happened here?" Daedalus wanted to know.

"At least one time too many."

Daedalus Rising

Icarus listened for a while longer, but became bored with the conversation after the story of the earthquake was through. He was no longer looking at the men as they spoke. He leaned over the rail and watched the movement of the morning sunlight on the water and the shore birds foraging for food and scurrying through the surf as the waves came in. They were free to go as they pleased, lucky birds. He was stuck on this ship. He grew impatient with his situation. He burned away the restlessness with motion, skipping around the ship while the two men talked. The skipping paces began to alternate with extended sliding steps and then with each rotation around the deck, he jumped to touch a spot in the rigging, high overhead and above the mast.

Daedalus and the sailor were engrossed in their conversation. The sailor spoke as if it was a foregone conclusion that he and Icarus would soon be going there. What a relief that was to hear, right along with the confirmation that there was still much rebuilding to be done.

When the king learned that there was a man who claimed to be Daedalus the architect on a ship in his harbor, he was delighted. King Minos was a rich and a powerful man with a need for a master builder. His beautiful palace with the high interior walls and supporting columns had been ravaged by the earthquake almost ten years before. First, the floors within the multilevel buildings collapsed and then the supporting walls caved in, crushing people, artwork and other treasures indiscriminately. Walls and buildings can be rebuilt and restored. But all the rest was lost. It was a terrible time. Everywhere Minos looked, he could still see the need for major repairs and restoration. There were few on the island with the skills to rebuild to his liking.

"How can you be sure that this man is really Daedalus the builder?" the king asked the captain, wanting to know all he could about the visitors.

"Because," the captain replied, "we had a disagreement during the voyage and the crew and I had to test his mettle. We tested him hard and learned his real name and that's as far as it went. When he did make a stand, he included the boy. I'll wager Icarus is his son, although he never said as much. The man has to be Daedalus."

The king thanked the captain and his crew for their efforts and invited them all to rest and to take a holiday in the city, once the builder and his son were brought to the palace. He assured the captain that if his passenger was indeed the master builder, then he and his crew would be well rewarded.

The captain wasted no time in returning to the harbor.

Later that day, after the sun went down, Icarus fell asleep on the deck. Now it was Daedalus who paced around the deck, unable to sleep and thinking about the day ahead. And he thought of the flight dream and wondered whether or not it would return. The thrill of the sensation of flight made a strong memory and he wanted it to come back. There was so much to look forward to.

Miles away King Minos also paced. Late into the night, he walked through the palace, mentally recording his ideas and plans. He was too excited to sleep. He wanted a new set of eyes to examine and review his plans. This could be a whole new phase of rebuilding. It would start right away. Assuming that the man in the harbor was really Daedalus and if he turned out to be as good as the stories that preceded him.

His throne room, once a place that exuded power and justice, was just not the same, ever since the earthquake. Repairs had been made, but they were not to his liking. Since the earthquake, when it was warm enough, he prefered to hold court and conduct his councils in one of the courtyards outside. His high backed stone throne was centered along the inner wall of a beautiful courtyard, adorned with flowers and alive with color. Behind the throne, mythic creatures on rolling hills were painted in a huge mural, done in the colors of the island, deep reds, blues and yellows. It was an elegant and striking space and it would be a fine place to meet the newcomers.

Daedalus Rising

The next morning, the captain was back on the ship, with new found affection and support for his captives. Giving each of them new clothes, something fit to wear before the king, he wished each of them good fortune. They were provided with plentiful provisions and two of the crew assigned the task of guiding them on their trek to the palace. Panos was one of the two. A small boat was on its way out into the deeper water to pick them up and take them into shore. While there was still time the captain took Daedalus aside from the others. He spoke with a quiet confidence and said quite unexpectedly, "You did well the other night. If you ever need a good ship again, think about us."

It surprised Daedalus that he could feel a sense of connection to this man who was now reaching out to him. So he smiled and nodded and said, "You'll be giving me back my money, right?"

The Captain just laughed.

Minutes later they stepped into the surf on the shore of the island. Sand had never before felt so good. Daedalus paused there, took off his sandals, dug his toes in and reveled in the moment. Icarus ran ahead and urged everyone to quickly follow. It was a momentous occasion for each of them, to move their legs and feet on the earth again after so many days on the ship.

The sleepy little cluster of low buildings was quiet. The inhabitants just waking up as they passed through, on their way to the road that led to the palace. It was a new day. The struggles and the fear on the ship, the sweat and endless waiting in the harbor, those things were past now. Some very promising unknowns lay ahead. The idea of turning back was inconceivable now. Just to have come this far felt like a gift and that was more than enough to be glad. Daedalus walked up the hillside on the hard packed earth, tears mixing with his sweat.

The road leading out of the village was wide enough for a two wheeled cart and easy to follow. It wound its way up to the top of the ridge between the high hills that ringed the harbor, where they had a clear, unobstructed view of their ship and the sea stretching out beyond. One of the guides pointed ahead to a distant landmark and marked their direction. Tree covered, rolling hills lay ahead of them and Daedalus was not sure he could pick out whatever it was that the sailor was describing, but that didn't matter. It was a sunny clear day and perfect for walking.

After a few more hours, they came to a high point along the trail that provided a view of a large city ahead. Terraced buildings draped across the flank of the hillside, clinging to the slope. At the bottom of the hill, a narrow river channel flowed through the picturesque valley.

"See the tallest buildings - there grouped in the center of the city?" asked Panos, "They are the palace."

Daedalus could see a complex of buildings, courtyards and open areas. The guide's descriptions from the day before were accurate enough. It was different from Athens, with its elevated Parthenon in the center of a crowded city, all surrounded by a defensive outer wall. This new city didn't have battlements. There was nothing to mark its outer edge except for the beginning of the adjoining fields.

Further along in their walk, Daedalus could see small sculptures placed at regular intervals along the top of the outer walls of the palace. They were all uniform in shape and at first, gave the appearance of a row of sentinels perched along the roof lines. Coming closer still to their destination, he could see that the sentinels were made in the outline of the horns of a bull and all facing slightly outward. To the newcomers the rows of horns made quite a statement. It was certainly a projection of power, much different from the defensive wall around Athens.

The road turned from packed earth to pavestones and grew wider. Soon, they were walking along a terraced road that overlooked the river, swelling its banks with runoff from the mountains. Then the road turned and went directly up the gentle slope to the city itself. As it twisted through neighborhoods and commercial areas, the high walls of the palace were lost from view.

Daedalus Rising

Eventually, they came to a large open hallway, formed by two rows of thick pillars holding up a long flat roof. The floor was covered in beautiful mosaic tile and Icarus slowed to trace the spiral patterns with his feet. While Icarus played with the tile, Daedalus looked up and through the red pillars to a beautiful fresco of rolling hills against a deep blue sky, painted upon the plaster surface of a wall at the far end of the hallway. The painting was protected from the elements by the overhang of a high roof with carved double horns at each end. Daedalus and Icarus both had to stop to take it all in. Their guides didn't hurry them and after a few more moments, all of them walked together through a wide open passageway. On the other side, a young guide with clean, smooth skin and much better attired than any of them, seemed to be waiting for them. Recognizing them, he bowed slightly and offered to take the guests the rest of the way. Daedalus and Icarus had entered the north entrance to the palace.

The True Story of Icarus

Chapter 11

King Minos

*"At the moment of commitment,
the universe conspires to assist you."*
~Johann Wolfgang von Goethe

With the guide on one side and Icarus on the other, Daedalus walked through a wide passage into the large central court and from there into a brilliant courtyard, festooned with flowers and beautiful rugs spread over stone floors. Oil lamps of hand wrought gold hung suspended from poles that ringed seven chairs arranged in a slight arc, closing off the far end. Of the seven perched upon the richly embroidered silk cushions, it was easy to see which of them was the most important, the man dressed in gold and white robes seated in the center chair. The one with the highest back, with curvilinear lines and carved from stone.

"So this is the king," thought Daedalus.

It was the most luxurious display of furnishings in the open air that Daedalus had ever seen. The robes that he and Icarus wore, new as they were, seemed out of place as he looked at the elegant men and women gathered in clusters around the courtyard in their vibrant colors. Servants came and went with silver trays laden with spices and tea. There was a table arrayed with the finest fruits and cheeses on the island. It was a gathering and it seemed as if everyone waited for an event to unfold. Icarus was more than a little off guard. He stood behind Daedalus and off to one side.

Motioning for them to wait, their guide entered the assembled gathered, nodded and exchanged glances as he made his way to the white haired man seated in the largest of the chairs. Heads turned in unison and the courtyard grew silent, eyes focused upon the strange man and the young boy. Soon the king nodded at them, recognized them and beckoned them forward. Icarus quickly lengthened his stride, to keep up. Together, they approached the king. As they walked those few steps, Daedalus felt the king's eyes taking him in and making the assessments he would feel compelled to make. Daedalus looked into his face, met the eyes and nodded with a half smile, reminding himself that he had spoken with the king of Athens many times and that this man was no different.

From his elevated perch, the king nodded again to Daedalus and welcomed him saying, "If you are Daedalus, then I know of your fame as an engineer and an architect. You are welcome on my island, for there is much need for your talents and abilities."

Daedalus replied, paraphrasing the words he had used on the deck of the ship just a few days before, saying "I am Daedalus, the builder and the architect. I served the king of Athens for many years. My work there speaks for itself. Icarus and I have traveled to your island to offer our services wherever they are needed to rebuild your city and your palace."

King Minos smiled and beckoned them with his open hand to look around. "It is a shell of what it once was. So many of the walls and pillars tumbled down and no one has found a way to rebuild it all. The main hall has no roof. How can you make these things right, when so many before you have failed?"

"I built many fine homes and temples in Athens and it is different there. I have brought ideas and techniques that your own builders do not have and I am seeing the palace for the first time, with a new perspective."

"My builders have tried, but there are many problems they cannot solve. It's been ten years since the earthquake. The main hall is still in ruins because the secret for building the roof has been lost. There is no light reaching the inner rooms and they flood when it rains."

"They can make their best efforts to restore what was there before. I am not bound by their preconceptions. Why limit the palace to being restored, when it could be recreated into something more than its former splendor." Daedalus confidently replied.

The king waited a bit to respond and then looked into the newcomer's face, wondering how much value to place upon his words and asking, "How long do you think that I should wait for you to prove your worth?"

"Give me one year to demonstrate the value of my ideas. In that time, you will know from the progress of the work, whether I have the skills to rebuild the palace to your satisfaction."

"A year goes by quickly. What if I am not pleased in that time?" the king asked.

"If you can give me one full year before passing judgment on the work, then you can do whatever it is that a king does," Daedalus replied.

Sensing that an agreement had been reached, King Minos smiled at both of them, acknowledging Icarus for the first time. "If you can do these things, you and your son are welcome on my island. You shall live in the palace and have a home in this city."

With those words, Daedalus understood why the palace was comprised of so many separate buildings. It was a complex of structures designed to house a community of people, many more than just one or two noble families and their servants. He and Icarus were included in that community. He could hardly believe what he heard. In a few short weeks, he had gone from being a prosperous builder in Athens, to a penniless man far from home. Now he was a prosperous builder again and this time with a young son.

He turned to Icarus and hugged him, sharing a moment of comfort and fulfillment, the satisfaction of a promise kept. He thought of the crew and the captain of the ship that brought them from Athens, relieving them of their remaining possessions along the way. Now they all served the same king. He smiled at the irony of it, realizing that if he had walked off that ship still disguised as a blind man, he would not have gained such a prompt audience with the king. What a delicious irony, he thought, that he had to lose everything, in order to get this far.

Icarus smiled right back at him, appreciating the moment in his own way. In the shared glance, it was understood that each felt very grateful and without question, it was all worth it. And on top of everything else, the king just recognized them as father and son. It was a blessing of sorts, albeit an unintentional one from the king's perspective. But still, it came from the king and that was enough.

Tea was brought and they drank together from crystal glasses. For a time, the king spoke and then other nobles followed, explaining their ideas about the work that remained. Daedalus listened and tried to learn as much as he could about these people. It was a pleasant and collegial exchange of ideas and never once did anyone ask Daedalus about his life in Athens or his reasons for leaving. But before the evening concluded the king made a point of leading him away and out of ear shot of anyone else of the other guests. Turning to him, the king's face grew hard as he stared into the eyes of the master builder and said: "I know why you left Athens and I know what happened to your apprentice. Serve me with devotion and I will forget your past. If you fail in that service, then both of your lives are forfeit."

Daedalus just returned the king's gaze, making no response.

The king waited another moment, relaxed a bit and continued, "That is enough for now. Your guide will show you the rooms where you will be living and the school Icarus will attend. Rest and refresh yourselves and return here in the morning. We will tour the palace and talk of things to come."

Chapter 12

Life In the Palace

*Our life evolves our character.
You find out more about yourself as you go on.
That's why it's good to be able
to put yourself in situations that will
evolve your higher nature rather than your lower.*
~Joseph Campbell, The Power of Myth

Their home was a large apartment with a veranda overlooking the valley, not far from the central courtyard. There were even servants to watch over their needs. It was their's for at least a year, or as long as the king was pleased. Then Daedalus and Icarus began to rebuild the pieces of their lives.

As it turned out, there were many lessons to be learned on the blank slates that were given them. At times, it seemed to Daedalus that it was easier to reconstruct a building than a life. The differences in the cultures made him very aware, sometimes, of how far away from home he was. The sets of habits and routines and perceptions that he brought along from Athens, did not always serve him here.

Icarus, however, at his young age, was a quick study in the art of adapting to his environment. Daedalus pondered and questioned why things and events were the way they were. More often than not, after some teasing or suggestion from Icarus, he would let go of his need to be in control of an outcome. He listened to the feedback he was getting, not just in his work, but also in his life. It was the easiest way to grow.

These were good times for both of them, times of growth and change. Sometimes, when it felt overwhelming, Daedalus tried to remember the flight dream. The memory of it always had a soothing effect. It was such a positive memory and remembering it, he would hope for the rest of the day to pass quickly and for night to come and for the dream to return. In those first few months on the island, his sleep came quickly, deep, restful and dreamless. Many days went by without even thinking of it and little by little the memory began to fade. And so it went for many days.

The reconstruction was no small undertaking. The city was connected to an intricate system of irrigation canals and aqueducts that brought water from the melting snow in the nearby mountains. Much of the water was collected in cisterns and spring chambers that were lined with water resistant plaster. Some was channeled into baths and pools and then allowed to run down through the gutters that lined the streets and even through some buildings and homes. This intricate system of culverts and drains provided the means for keeping the city both clean and cool in the hot summer months.

That was the way of it, before the earthquake. The aftershocks that followed broke apart many of the carefully constructed canals and drains and then water flooded relentlessly, caused much damage, until it could be damned up or the flows diverted at the sources in the high mountain streams and lakes.

The same aftershocks caused many of the higher walls in the palace itself to fall and the floors to collapse; leaving many of the once smooth roof lines broken and open to the sky. The island had a beautiful, warm climate. This allowed open air and increased light to pour in through the damaged roofs, bringing light and warmth to many places that were once darker and drearier.

Of course, during the rainy months, the damage could no longer be excused as a functional skylight and in those times, a hole in the roof was no more than a hole. Water fell into the rooms below and collected in streams and rivulets, following descending courses to the lowest levels of the city. Pools collected in murky corners, which later spawned all kinds of insects and generated peculiar smells, the smells of a city in decay. Teams of servants and slaves spent countless hours since the earthquake, draining the palace and the city and cleaning up after each new storm.

The lore of the city now included stories of how long lines of people formed around the uninvited pools of water and drained them by filling their ornate and colorful urns, passing the water from the low places to the closest outside wall. Minos and the council were even considering a commission to paint a mural to commemorate this new part of their history on one of the long palace walls.

Notwithstanding all those efforts, there was a dark, wet and dreary place below the palace where the teams of water bearers would not go. Many years before, the palace was constructed over an entrance to a large cavern, created by the natural course of erosion into the underlying limestone. In those early days, the caverns were used for underground storage, a warehouse for food and water and other supplies against future shortages. Tunnels and underground passages were constructed for expansion and to make a proper connection between the palace and the caverns. As the years past and the city prospered and expanded, warehouses were built above ground at different locations to meet the growing needs of the population. In time, the caverns were given over to a different use.

King Minos found that this system of isolated and inaccessible caverns was the ideal place to contain thieves, miscreants and other undesirables. It was a dark maze of blind passages and twisting paths, the shadow side of the beautiful palace and city and it came to be known as the labyrinth.

Daedalus Rising

After the earthquake, much of the water which flowed into the palace, drained down into the labyrinth and it gradually filled with water and debris. The water stagnated and became putrid and the labyrinth became a dreary, fearful place that could not support life. The lavish abundance of the fragrant flowers in the courtyards above had more purpose than beauty and visual appeal alone. For the palace to be restored, the labyrinth had to be drained.

And the task had fallen to Daedalus to reconstruct these things to the king's liking. He spent many hours touring the city and discovering how all of the systems fit together. He met often with the king and the nobles and all the people that lived in the palace, to learn how they lived and what was important to them. After a time, he began to make designs and to construct plans for the work that was needed and then that which would beautify as well. When he finally presented the plans, the king was most receptive. Soon laborers, servants, materials and slaves were assigned to his projects and the work began in earnest.

In a short time, there was no doubt that the work of restoring the city was enjoying a resurgence. King Minos enjoyed the visibility of touring the city to watch the progress and he was pleased. So pleased, in fact, that the first year came and quickly went, without anyone even raising the question of whether or not Daedalus should be allowed to continue.

Icarus had things to do as well. He had to relearn how to live life as a young boy, one with enough food to eat and friends to play with, a school to attend and a father to care that all these things were happening in the right order. The lessons that he had learned in Athens, how to survive as a beggar and a thief, did not serve him here. Those were the lessons of surviving in scarcity and here on the island, relying on them seemed to invite scorn and ridicule. In time, he decided that it was best to leave them behind. Just as Daedalus had to learn about listening and communication and how to accept the ways of this new land, Icarus needed to learn how to thrive in the prosperity that was all around him, instead of accepting mere survival.

They were not always easy lessons. There were times, particularly in those early days on the island, when Daedalus found himself dealing with an angry or brooding Icarus, who found himself in some kind of trouble. It was a new role for Daedalus and after a few false starts, he was able to learn that he couldn't and shouldn't try to fix everything, only things made of stone, earth and wood. Hearts and egos mended according to their own schedules. The better outcomes seemed to happen when he was able to persuade Icarus to talk about his obstacle, to give voice to his pain or his fear or his anger and then encourage him to find a way to resolve his own difficulty.

Daedalus remembered very well his own dark times back in Athens, when he had needed to be alone. He knew to give Icarus enough space at times like that, but he also found the right time to give comfort and say, "You are my golden child. There is no one like you in the whole wide world."

Slowly and surely their lives on the island were shaped into new habits and routines. It did not take long before Icarus sounded and acted like every other boy his age on the island. As his confidence grew, he put aside the barriers and the defenses that he had once used to protect himself as an orphan in Athens, replacing them with an energy and a zest for life that attracted others.

Icarus was not drawn to concentrate over puzzles or to use inventive skill, things that Daedalus enjoyed. It was clear to anyone with eyes that he did not want to follow Daedalus' path as a builder. He liked games and was high-spirited. He wanted to spend his time in sports with others his age, to hunt and fish in the mountains and to camp on the beaches along the coast. Daedalus began to take great pride in watching Icarus do these things and sometimes he found himself wanting to share in them. They seemed to compliment and support his own achievements as an architect and builder. As Icarus grew in size and stature, the two of them grew more and more accustomed to the emotional thread that had woven their lives together and the relationship grew and deepened.

Daedalus Rising

These were good times for Daedalus. His days certainly had their challenges. There were always new tasks to complete in the work of putting the palace back together, obstacles to work through. As always, he took great pride in his work, but it was not an obsession. There was a balance to his life that he had not known before. Now, he looked forward to a hopeful future. Daedalus felt content.

Chapter 13

Waiting for the Dream

Let yourself be silently drawn
By the stronger pull
Of what you really love.

~Rumi

After a time, Daedalus began to forget about the flight dream. He filled his days with ideas and experiences of being a father and the memory of the dream simply faded. Perhaps he no longer needed or wanted the exhilaration or the sense of vitality that it once carried. A day would pass without even thinking of it, then two and then a week. Little by little, it lost its influence, turning into something remote and inaccessible. It became something that had happened once, a moment in the sun and now it was gone. Their days in the palace on the other hand, were quite full, marked by incremental increases in the length and sturdiness of Icarus' legs, increasing grey in Daedalus' beard and steady progress in the reconstruction of the palace and the city.

Daedalus designed and built an elegant system of wooden beams to transfer the weight of the new roofs to the vertical columns that supported them. Now when it rained, the water was channeled into gutters and drains, which led to a complex system of filters, cisterns and ponds. More than that the new roof design provided regularly spaced openings, an early form of skylight, constructed over shafts of open air that were built around the backs of many buildings, allowing sunlight and warmth onto balconies and to garden areas and with more drains and clay pipes to carry any rain water away.

While that work progressed, a site was selected for another crew to construct a tunnel, drilling up and into the labyrinth from below. Once the connection was made, gravity took over, freeing much of the watery mix of sediment and debris that filled it. Then the far reaches of the caverns were explored, extending its former reach. Bars were installed at openings and a formidable door set at the entrance. Soon, it became widely known that the labyrinth was back in use, regaining its former notoriety and once more symbolizing the shadow side of the king's power.

After a few years, the palace was restored to its former splendor and more. The pride of Daedalus' restoration work was his design and construction of a grand staircase. From a broad balcony that overlooked the entire valley, three stories of wide stone steps descended around an open shaft onto the eastern side of the central court, a portal for grand entrances by musicians, dancers and other performers. It was an engineering feat and a thing of aesthetic beauty.

On the open side, the steps were supported by a series of deep red and blue columns and on the other, large colorful murals were painted from floor to ceiling in rich patterns, depicting the natural beauty of the island with its flowers, animals, marine life and birds. The huge steps were slanted slightly away from the center, to drain into a stone trough that ran along the outer edge, deep and continuous enough to hold a controlled cascade of water. This flow would eventually make its way to a complex system of vertical shafts built into the outside walls, all joining into a single channel that created a water fall as it flowed out of the palace wall, feeding a small pond several meters below.

The city was becoming, once again, a work of art and a magnet for adventurers and travelers. Traders and merchants from North Africa and all over the Mediterranean returned to their homelands and told of the detail of the craftsmanship and the beauty of the art. Many others were drawn to see it.

Minos, of course, became the envy of all the other Mediterranean kings. He was lavish in his praise for the architect and engineer who designed and reconstructed his palace and his city.

Daedalus was proud of the restoration also. His reputation as an architect and builder was even more renowned than before. Once again, through some combination of talent and perseverance, he achieved personal success as a builder of stone, wood and earth, this time for King Minos. And this time, he was much more content. He had a personal life and it was not in opposition to his professional one.

With the work on the palace coming together so well, Daedalus sometimes found himself watching the sun go down and reflecting on his journey since leaving Athens. So much had happened. Under the starry sky, he reflected on the man he was back in Athens and wondered where that man had gone. The Athenian version of himself was a stranger now. It was not just Icarus that had changed. Both had grown, his own was just not as apparent as the physical changes the boy was going through.

"What could possibly be next?" he wondered to himself.

The days rolled by fast. He marked their passing by the completed projects, all within a larger plan or design and everything in rhythm with the available daylight hours. The goals he set for himself since coming to the island were met. He had kept his commitments to Icarus and to the king and now he found himself wondering if there was still more to do and to be. His life seemed to be on a wide plateau and he was as high and as far as he could go.

One evening, while sitting on his veranda and staring at the night sky, he remembered the flight dream. The one that came on the first night in the harbor, while he slept on the deck of the ship. He tried to remember the small details, but they didn't come so easily. What he could remember was the sheer splendor of it and the effect that it seemed to have over him. He thought about how good it would be to have that kind of drive again. He thought about how good it would be to be able to tap into that reservoir of energy one more time. There was so much personal growth when he had the dream in his life. He wanted to know that feeling again. He looked into the night sky and hoped for the dream to come back.

"How is it possible that after all the things that have happened and everything I've done, that a dream could seem the best and the most sublime experience of all?" The energy of it must have seeped into his cells. That night, he lay awake in the darkness, letting the memories spill out and overflow into the waking moments of the night. But the dream did not come.

During the days that followed, he lost himself in his habits and his work routines and not think of it, but at night the longing for the dream came back. Before falling asleep, he would lie awake and savor the memory of it for a while. The dream itself stayed away, while the longing for it remained. It was an irresistible attraction, a magnetism that held the possibility of his own perfection. He wanted very much to know that feeling again.

The True Story of Icarus

Chapter 14

The Foe

*And these tend inward to me,
and I tend outward to them,
and such as it is to be of these more or less I am,
and of these one and all, I weave the song of myself.*
~Walt Whitman, Leaves of Grass

King Minos was known throughout the island as the lawgiver and he was. It was during his reign that written language, something that had been developing for generations as a means of accounting for and distributing quantities of stored food and other materials, was expanded in its usage to include the making a written record of the rulings that he and his council made in resolving the many disputes that came before them. As the records accumulated, they were compiled and summarized into a code of laws that became of the standard, more or less, for the people of the island to live by and to conduct their affairs.

Commerce thrived in this predictable and stable environment. Trade flourished, generating wealth and a growing awareness of their own abundance in the people of the island. Between the natural beauty and the thriving economy, many outsiders were attracted to the island; some of them fine artists, artisans and musicians. Daedalus and Icarus certainly had not been the only ones. It was the growing wealth of the community that had financed the rebuilding of the city after the earthquake, just as it financed and supported a formidable navy. These ships extended his reach far beyond the island itself. And here too, Minos ruled with authority.

It was not surprising then, that King Aegeus of Athens and King Minos had a history. In earlier days, when both men were much younger, there was a fierce naval battle between the two states. Even now the Athenian King paid an annual tribute to Minos so that Athenian ships bound for Egypt, or some other part of the Mediterranean, could sail safely past the island. There were two parts to the tribute. First, was the requisite amount of gold. The second called for seven young men and seven young women, the best and brightest of Athens, to come each year and serve at the pleasure of King Minos. None of them ever returned to Athens.

One by one, Minos would tire of them, blaming each for some irritation or disappointment. Sometimes, the offender would be sold like so much merchandise and carried off to another land; sometimes he would confine them to the dank depths of the labyrinth, the maze whose reconstruction Daedalus had overseen. It was not a place from which any returned.

Every year since their arrival when the time came for the young Athenians to be brought before the king and placed into service, Daedalus remembered who he was and where he came from. It didn't matter that he had once been driven away. Athens was his home. His roots were there and it was impossible not to identify with and sympathize with the young Athenians.

He did not know how to look away and each year he felt worse about it. Their mistreatment by the king was a growing source of contention between the man he was and the man he was becoming. But it was not something he felt comfortable discussing with anyone. It might not be safe. Minos had warned them long ago that they were welcome on the island as long as they each served him. For years now, Daedalus had kept his compassion for the young Athenians to himself. He stuffed it inside mostly, but it came out occasionally, in shared thoughts with Icarus.

The True Story of Icarus

Sometimes, this kind of talk created its own conflict in Icarus. Icarus had spent about half of his life in Athens and half on the island; to him, there was no doubt which had been the better half. Since their arrival, he concentrated all of his energy to adapting to the ways of the islanders, their mannerisms, speech and culture. He had wanted nothing more than to recreate himself so that he would be just like all the other boys on the island. And mostly, he had done it.

Outside of the home, Icarus moved and spoke with the air and the sound of someone who had lived on the island all his life. Inside the home with Daedalus, he wore a slightly different persona. They usually spoke in the old dialect, especially when his father would go on and on describing the travails of the young Athenians and the excesses of Minos. Usually, he listened without responding very much. It was his way of living in two places; the world of his peers and that of his home. He thrived in both.

Over the years, Daedalus tried to rationalize that he himself had been driven away from Athens, so what did their fate matter. Other times, he was more honest with himself and recognized that the king's will was not something that he wanted to challenge. After all, he had a city to restore and repair and a son to raise. They shared a home together and it was important to preserve that home. He had made a promise and out of that commitment he had grown accustomed to the routines and habits of their lives. He was not willing to place that stability at risk. So every year, he endured the plight of the young Athenians, but each year it was more difficult for him to turn his head and look away.

One way that he coped with his growing dilemma was to avoid it. For several years, just before the Athenians arrived, he and Icarus left the city. They would go on a long adventure together, camping and roaming the countryside. They hunted and fished and had glorious times, living off the island's abundance. Together they explored the lands that surrounded the palace, the thinly sprinkled settlements of farmers and shepherds, fishermen and pirates.

Daedalus Rising

During these adventures, they sat by their fire at night under a starry sky and told and retold their stories. Icarus always had new ones about his friends and sports and school. And they had the stories they shared, the memories of their times together, stories they could still laugh about, no matter how many times they were told. The stories commemorated the growth and change in their enduring relationship. They trusted each other and it showed in the ease and comfort they enjoyed in each other's company. They knew each other so well, that when Daedalus would drop his voice and begin to speak in somber tones, Icarus knew that the topic was going to be something about the Athenians and the injustice of their treatment. Even away from the palace on their trips, Daedalus could not or would not forget.

Icarus had not forgotten that he too had come from Athens. He certainly identified with the young slaves and he understood that what was happening to them was wrong. But he also loved his friends and identified with the people in the capitol city. Besides it was like this when they arrived. That was just the way it was and there was nothing he could do about it, even if he wanted to.

His years on the island were the best of his life and he wanted to keep it that way. His friends and even his teachers were all born on the island, something that he could never be. This difference made him stand out sometimes. So he was used to working at fitting in. And because he felt like he had to try just a little harder than anyone else to feel like he belonged, when he was alone with Daedalus under the stars by the fire, sometimes he would admit to his own discontentment. He spoke of how easy it was to fit in and be part of the group when everything was going well. But when something went wrong, when an item turned up missing or a teacher became overwhelmed by the stress of the day, then the islanders would find a way to remind him that he was not one of them, that he was from Athens and the Athenian son of an Athenian father.

The True Story of Icarus

Many times, Daedalus watched his son struggle with this desire to be accepted. Many times over the years, he marveled at Icarus' willingness to keep swimming upstream, but Icarus never seemed to tire of it. Now away from the city and listening to him express that sense of being an outsider, of not being fully connected, Daedalus had to wonder how different would Icarus' life be when he was gone, compared to the young Athenians that were forced to come to the island each year.

When they were out of the city and on one of their adventures, it was easy to talk of these things long into the night as they sat by the fire, of the differences in the cultures, of wanting to be independent and of wanting to belong. There was security in their isolation under a brilliant canopy of stars and so far away from the palace. But even though they both felt safe discussing these things, Daedalus had not shared his deepest fear, the thought that Icarus might someday become a target, enslaved by Minos and imprisoned in the labyrinth.

This year with Icarus mostly grown, Daedalus could not help but remember the words he spoke and the promise made all those years ago back in the harbor in Athens to a young boy that he hardly knew. "If you come with me, then I will keep you safe and see that you are never hungry." Daedalus smiled at the thought of the fullness of the years that had past since then. He was so pleased with the outcome, so pleased with the man that Icarus was becoming. It gave him a sense of satisfaction with his own life and because of that, he was grateful that the opportunity had come along all those years ago and that he had stayed committed to it.

Eventually, they returned to the palace together, Icarus to his friends, his school and his sports and Daedalus to his work. Icarus' growth and maturation had matched the pace of the restoration work on the palace. From Daedalus' perspective, both were nearly complete, even though Minos had a way of finding new projects that needed his attention. He made no secret of his pleasure with Daedalus' work. Lately, there was talk among the king and the counsel about designing and building a new temple complex. Minos, of course, would want it to be the finest anywhere.

But so far, there was no joy in it for Daedalus, no inspiration at the thought of this new project. With the passing of the year, he found himself less and less inclined to take on new tasks. He even began to dream now about returning to his homeland. In these dreams with all of the tasks that he had undertaken for the king completed, he departed from the island with much fanfare and ceremony on the same ship and crew that first brought them, this time with riches and fame. In the dreams, he traveled alone and he searched everywhere for Icarus, never finding him. But in the latest version of the dream Icarus was found. He was one of the next group of slaves from Athens.

After that, Daedalus resolved that he could not go on this way any longer. This year it would be different. This year, before the arrival of the Athenians, he would go to King Minos and intercede on their behalf. Minos would listen to him. They knew each other too well.

In his mind, their fates were all intertwined, the young Athenians, Icarus and himself. They were all connected somehow, threads in the same fabric. Even though he was confident about his own ability to remain in the king's favor, at least as long as he was healthy and could build, what would happen to Icarus when he was gone? Wasn't it just a matter of time before Icarus fell into disfavor? And for that matter, what if he was no longer healthy? Was there any guarantee that he himself would not end up entombed in the labyrinth?

"How long can I continue to let Minos control our destinies?" Daedalus wondered.

From what he had seen of the king's excesses, Minos was not a good choice for holding that kind of power over either of them. The alternative, as Daedalus saw it, would be to step into that role for himself, and become a citizen king and take back control of his own life. At the same time, he might also model that lesson for Icarus. Daedalus didn't know how to effect that

The True Story of Icarus

kind of initiation. If there was a ritual for it, he certainly hadn't experienced it when he was growing up, so he had no guides or lessons of his own to draw from. But he was sure that he was the one to speak for all of them, even if it meant challenging the king.

It was comforting to remember that he had taken a similar chance at least once before. Back in Athens, a much younger man, he risked everything in order to sail into an unknown sea and pursue his dream of being an architect on this island. For a time, he found satisfaction here, but that has changed. It was no longer enough. Once again, he found himself pondering how best to leave an old life behind in order to move into a new one for himself and for Icarus.

After leaving Athens behind, he eventually found fulfillment in the pursuit of his own dreams. Along the way, he found Icarus, or perhaps, Icarus had found him. Either way, he was then able to fulfill a new dream of creating a safe and supportive home for both of them. It was much more than just an occupation, even more than being a father. He was a provider, a teacher and a model, an example of positive masculine energy. That brought its own kind of fulfillment. Over the years, he demonstrated his ability to serve others well, first the Athenian king and now king Minos. He wondered if he could provide the same service to himself and be his own king.

Chapter 15

Confrontation

*It is not because things are difficult that we do not dare,
It is because we do not dare, that they are difficult.*
　　　　　　　　　　　　　　　　　　~Seneca

The courtyard was framed on three sides by high walls. Two large griffins in shades of red, orange and yellow painted within a pastoral scene faced one another from opposite walls. A semi-oval of chairs was arrayed before them, the king's stone chair in the center.

It was late spring and the king held court among the beautiful gardens, just the way he did when Daedalus first came to the island all those years ago. Daedalus was anxious about their meeting. Many times he had spoken with the man about projects that the king sponsored. This time the perspectives were different. It was Daedalus this time with a different agenda, his own and asking the king to change. Entering the courtyard, he approached purposefully, wondering why it was that the king felt the need to elevate his chair above all the others. Had it been so high off the ground the first time that they met? But that was so long ago. Who can remember such details?

As he walked into the courtyard, Daedalus looked at the flowers, the mural and the sky with appreciation, as if seeing them for the first time. The king watched as his architect approached. There was no ease in the man's step today. So the king watched and waited, trying to read his attitude from all the silent cues before any words were spoken. After reaching the

The True Story of Icarus

throne, Daedalus gazed at him for a moment, smiling with the ease of a man who recognized another man from their years of association, albeit without mutuality. He was ready, determined to launch into the subject that was heavy on his mind.

The king spoke first, as was his custom and sensing the architect's unease, tried to establish a connection. "Welcome, Daedalus. A lovely spring day isn't it? Have you come to discuss ideas for the design of the new temple?"

"No. That is not why I want to speak with you."

"Then what brings you to court today? You appear to be troubled?"

"I am. All the work that was done in restoring the labyrinth, I regret it now. Were you planning, even then, to use it for the killing of Athenian slaves each year?" he asked, looking right into the king's eyes. "If I had known of that intent, my plans would have been different."

"Are you feeling competing loyalties today, my friend?" asked the king calmly, making a palliative smile.

"There could already be another ship on its way right now, carrying gold for your coffers and more Athenians into your service. Why not spare their lives? Let them return to their homes. There would be no disgrace in it, because they have done nothing wrong. Their deaths would be an injustice."

The king said nothing and looked off into space.

"King Aegeus would still pay. Be satisfied with just the gold. There are so many servants already. What is there to lose by letting these go."

Minos silently shifted his gaze to the master builder, not understanding where all this was coming from. He thought to himself, "Who is this man today? Yesterday, he was my builder. Today he wants to be my advisor. What has changed for him, I wonder?"

On another day, Minos might have been angered by this turn of events, but he valued Daedalus' service and wanted it to continue. So he chose to turn away from the angry fire that was beginning to smolder in his spleen, allowing Daedalus to make the point that he apparently needed to make. Many people came before him and the council to resolve their disputes. He knew from long experience that the decisions were better when he remained emotionally detached from the outcome. It was not always an easy thing. Clearly the man before him had a lot on his mind, so the king prompted him.

"You are well paid master builder. Why are you not satisfied? Why can't you just be content with your pay, without troubling me with these questions?"

"I am troubled over the lives of the young Athenians, wasted in my labyrinth, the one that lies right under this palace," came the reply.

Hearing Daedalus refer to the labyrinth as his own raised the king's ire. His blood began to rise. The anger he had once easily dismissed was now knocking at the gate of his temperance and he lashed out sarcastically.

"With your past, master builder, I am surprised to learn that watching Athenians die is such a problem for you." Minos paused.

The two men stared fixedly at one another. And the king continued, "But no matter, I won't change. If I stop the killing, then the king of Athens will know that I am getting soft with age." Then shifting into a strident voice, "That is a perception that I will not allow."

Daedalus could feel the rage carried within the words. It washed over him, down his shoulders, his arms and legs and into the earth. Better to sway in this wind than resist it, he thought to himself.

In the throne room, the king had all the power. Daedalus knew he had nothing to gain and much to lose if he responded out of his own anger. He took a breath and reconnected with his own purpose, drawing from that strength. Then he continued on a slightly different tack.

"My work here is finished. Your palace is restored. When I first arrived on this island, I promised to serve you well and I have done that. Now I am ready to return to my home."

The True Story of Icarus

Finally he gets to the point, thought Minos to himself. Sensing that he was back in control, the king grew calmer and picked up the thread of the conversation.

"And what of your son? He has grown up in my palace. The only life he knows is on this island. And from what I have learned, his memories of Athens are not good ones. You Daedalus, have made this island his home. Are you ready to leave him behind or will he go with you?"

It was something he had not even considered and the words struck a deep chord, taking him aback. "He will go his own way when it is time," replied Daedalus altogether unsure of himself. At the mention of Icarus though, he was reminded of the king's indiscriminate power. It made him defensive. He did not trust the king on the subject of Icarus' future and he turned the subject back on himself.

"If I stay as your architect on this island, will you stop the torment of the Athenian slaves?"

"Are we back to that again!" demanded Minos, furious with this renewed attempt to take on an advisory role. The king let the storm of his anger boil over; glaring at Daedalus, he rose to his feet.

"You cannot stop being my builder, anymore than I can stop what happens to the Athenians. Your truth, master builder, is that you can no more go back to Athens than you can fly. I rule the land. And I rule the sea."

The king paused for moment and then continued, deliberately now.

"There are three reasons why you will stay on my island. First; you have no where else to go. Years ago you left Athens in shame. To try to return now is folly. What are you thinking? What makes you think they will have you? Second, you and Icarus are living a comfortable life in my court and you can not replace that anywhere. And third, as I told you when you first arrived on this island, you and Icarus are welcome, as long as each of you serve me. When that ceases for either one of you, then both of your lives are forfeit."

Daedalus Rising

Daedalus said nothing. His eyes were cast onto the floor and his shoulders slumped, a picture of defeat.

Having vented his anger, the old king sat back down exhausted. He paused and looked over at Daedalus, trying to catch his eye while he recovered his own breath. Before speaking again, he calmed himself. Now that the challenge by his builder was overcome, he could afford to be generous. Trying to smile, he opened the palms of his hands and then, in lower, subdued tones he even affected a submissive air casting his next words in an imploring tone.

"Daedalus, be reasonable. No where else will you have this kind of opportunity to do the work you want to do. You're a builder, the best on the island and there is so much more to be done. I can give you the materials and all the labor you could want. We have done so much together, you and I, in rebuilding this city. Look around you and see! And it can be even greater! Take Icarus and leave on the long holiday you take each year. By the time you come back, the young Athenians will be gone. You and Icarus will return to your life in the palace. Then you will begin your real work on the Temple of the Earth Goddess. It is yours to design and build from start to finish. This could be your life's work, your masterpiece."

This was not at all the outcome that Daedalus had come for, not what he had expected. He actually felt himself being won over. Part of him was inspired by the king's words. Daedalus wanted the comfort and security of his habits and routines. Part of him very much wanted to do the work on the new temple. In stunned silence, he looked up at the king and their eyes met. He wanted to tell him that he needed some time to consider, but when he opened his mouth to speak, the king cut him off with a wave of his hand. Minos looked straight at him with dark, intense eyes. Then he dropped his voice and spoke in a flat, emotionless tone.

"Now go. Before I tire of this conversation."

Chapter 16

Another Leap of Faith

I tramp a perpetual journey.
My signs are a rain-proof coat
and good shoes and a staff cut from the woods,
no friend of mine takes his ease in my chair,
I have no chair, nor church, nor philosophy;
I lead no one to a dinner-table or library or exchange,
but each man and each woman of you I lead upon a knoll,
my left hand hooks you round the waist,
my right hand points to landscapes of continents,
and a plain public road.
~Walt Whitman, Leaves of Grass

Daedalus walked for a long time that evening, leaving the city and following the cobblestone course of the river road. He thought about the words he and the king had spoken to one another. In retrospect, it was quite clear that neither one of them had listened to the other. Daedalus remonstrated to himself, thinking that he should have tried harder to find some common ground. It would not be an easy subject to bring up again. The king's position on the Athenian slaves was very clear and so was this offer to build the new temple and all of it said in the presence of the council. Minos would not lightly reconsider either one of them and now the two unrelated subjects were linked. If Daedalus began making designs for the new construction, many would regard it as acquiescence to the treatment of the slaves.

The road he walked along led to the proposed building site for the new temple. He stopped for a while and looked over the land, remembering the dream that came to him one night long ago, when he slept on the courtyard of his old home in Athens. Daedalus remembered the tablet and the promise that was made, that he would receive a gift, a great gift, something that would set him apart from all other men. Was it just a dream or was there really a promise out there, waiting to be fulfilled?

A few years before, he considered that Icarus coming into his life might have been the gift. Before that, when they first arrived on the island, he thought that the gift might have been the chance to work for king Minos. Now Daedalus was sure that Minos was something all right, but not a gift; he saw very clearly that Minos was just another man following his own dreams. He just happened to be the king, so he believed that his dreams carried a lot of weight. As for Icarus, he too was learning to demonstrate his willfulness. The child was growing up, asserting his individuality more and more. One day, he too would leave. He was not a gift that could belong to another. Daedalus wanted much more than that for his son.

Daedalus had to understand that if there was a gift at all, then he probably had not received it yet. Unless he somehow missed it and now the chance was gone. But there were many other things to think about this night. It was not that he was unhappy. He had a home and a job and his health and a family too, albeit an unconventional one. Why then, was he so discontented, so out of balance? Maybe he was just too busy, too occupied with the issues and expectations of others. That's how he felt about the offer to build the new temple, another opportunity to stay busy and preoccupied. It was a chance for him to fulfill king Minos' dream. Hadn't he done that for long enough? What about his own dreams?

The True Story of Icarus

While Daedalus mused, the palace buzzed with the talk of the days events.

"Did you see how angry the king became when the builder questioned his treatment of the Athenian slaves?"

"Not so angry as I've seen before."

"Did you see how the king handled Daedalus when he told him that he wanted to return to his native Athens? Daedalus is lucky he didn't end up in the labyrinth himself."

"Maybe he knows a secret way out and doesn't care."

"The king was angry enough to put him away for awhile. But he didn't. Minos is the king. He wouldn't take anything that Daedalus was selling."

"Nothing will change and that will be the end of it. Right?"

Late that night, Daedalus walked back to their apartment by the main courtyard. It was very late, but he couldn't sleep. He began making preparations for their trip, packing their backpacks, their sleeping gear, cooking utensils, fishing poles, knives and bows, taking everything they would need to sustain themselves on the land.

Icarus could not sleep either. Late into the night, a troubled Daedalus spoke to Icarus about what happened. Icarus had already heard several versions of the story, but he wanted to hear his father tell it.

Daedalus spoke of the pleasure that he found in the completion of his work on the palace and in the keeping of his promise to Icarus. Now, he wanted someday to return to Athens and more than that, he no longer wanted to watch the Athenian slaves go to their doom each year. So he told the king how he felt. He ended by describing the king's closing words, that they could no sooner leave the island than fly. Then he told Icarus how it felt to hear the king repeat his old threats; that both of their lives were forfeit, if either failed in their service.

"So what do we do now?"

"Well, one thing we could do is to stay on the island and make the best of it."

Daedalus Rising

"Why not stay? The island is my home."

"We have time to figure this out. Minos expects us to leave for a few weeks on our annual vacation, maybe even a few months. No one will question how much time we take. Let's just go and roam the island again together. Get away from all this."

"But will we return?"

"There are other places you know."

"You just want to go back to Athens."

"I understand that it is comfortable and secure here. This is the life you know. But how long can it last? When the temple is completed and Minos has no further use for us, what will happen to us then."

"I don't know, but that will be years from now. I will still be a young man."

"Yes. You can be so much, anything you choose, really. But listen to me. As I see it, if we stay on the island, we live our lives like tethered eagles. Minos lets us fly around a little, soaring over the palace from time to time, but we are stuck here, always tied by a very comfortable tether held by the king. There would never be any more freedom for you and I, than Minos will allow."

"What if I decide to stay?"

"You can do that. I will not deter you if that is your choice, but as I see it, that way does not end well. You know what eventually happens to Athenians on this island. We serve at the pleasure of Minos and that is as much of a life as we get. You and I have been fortunate. We live amongst the nobles of the island, birds in a gilded cage, as long as Minos appreciates and wants my work as his architect and engineer. It is comfortable here, even beautiful at times. But it is still a cage. One that belongs to Minos and it will only last as long as his interest lasts. What about you, Icarus? When I am gone? What will you do to set yourself apart so that you get better treatment than the other Athenians that come before Minos each year?"

"Father, I have no idea what I want to do in five years, or ten, or even one. What I know, is that I am happy now. The future will take care of itself."

"Then let's go and make room for that to happen, somewhere off of this island. That way you may actually get to have a future of your own."

"Why not just go off together and explore the island again. When that's over we can come back and live the way we've been living."

"That's what Minos expects us to do. What about his daughter?" teased Daedalus in reply. "You could marry her. That would ensure your future. Maybe mine, as well." Daedalus laughed seeing the discomfort spreading across his son's face.

"She will marry someone rich and powerful, you know that."

"Only because Minos will control that, as well."

Icarus didn't respond. He didn't want to have a conversation with his father about his blossoming and sometimes intense interest in women. Daedalus smiled and mercifully took the discussion in another direction.

"Icarus, since leaving Athens all those years ago, we have lived together as father and son. I could not stay in Athens any longer. My life was in ruin and everyone seemed against me. I decided to take a chance then. I knew nothing about this island, only that there had once been a substantial earthquake. I had hope that I could make a new life here as a builder, but little more than that. It was a step into the unknown. And just as I stood at that threshold alone and ready to jump, you appeared and we made the journey together. We left behind everything we had ever known. Since then, we have followed along the same path together. Now we are rapidly coming to another decision point, you and I, alot like the one back in Athens. But no one is forcing us this time. Instead, it's just the right thing to do. We can stay in the palace and go on as we always have, at the whim of the king. Or we can start making our own choices." Daedalus paused, trying to judge how deep the words were going.

"I don't want to go back to Athens. There is nothing for me there. And I don't understand why you would want to go there either," said Icarus.

"I'm not sure where exactly I want to go. Maybe it's not Athens after all. All is know is that I can't stay here."

Daedalus tilted his head back, as if looking for some kind of answer to the questions. Then, turning back to Icarus, he said, "I'm saying that we should leave the island, you and I, so that each of us, especially you, can have a real future. I fear for us here. We are both destined for the king's labyrinth, unless we choose another path. Come with me again. You're right. Athens is not the only option. It's my frame of reference and it's what I know. But there are other places and we can go anywhere. For me, Icarus, it is not the destination that is so important. What matters, is that the journey offers hope for both of us.

"You are so young, Icarus, so strong and vital, such a beautiful son. There is no other time in your life when you will have this much freedom and so many opportunities. You must use these things for your own advantage. If you don't, then you can be sure that someone else will. You can go anywhere, be anyone, do anything; you have only to choose. Here in the palace, you will never be more, have more, do more, than Minos will permit. Come with me. The journey will make you a man. We can find a way off the island. I know we can. Think of your life. Think of what you can do."

Icarus thought about the words, remembering a time long ago, back in the streets of Athens, when Daedalus first proposed that they go on a journey together. He was doing it all over again, making the same proposition. But back then, his life had been nothing but hardship after his mother was gone. He could still remember how she sounded and what it felt like when she was around. He could also remember being hungry and the feeling of having nothing to lose. That had made Athens an easy place to leave. That first journey across the sea had been a gift. Daedalus had given him that gift and now he was offering to make him a man, whatever that meant. Was it the same as before, another leap into the unknown? At least Daedalus had always been there, just like he promised that he would. And he was right about the king. He would do whatever suited him.

The True Story of Icarus

Icarus smiled at the father who made him want to look into his own future. With a laugh, he repeated the same words that he said as a young boy, ready to flee a city that had not been kind, "When do we leave?"

"Soon. There are several things I want to finish before I go," replied Daedalus. "So take the next day to prepare and say your goodbyes. We can depart after that, the same way we always do. No one can think that there is anything out of the ordinary about this adventure. We'll walk out of the palace, right under the king's nose and with everyone believing that they know of our plans. We just won't mention the part about searching for a boat once we get far enough away. We're agreed, then?"

"I can be ready to leave in another day. There are friends, teachers and places that I want to see one more time."

"Of course. But you can't tell anyone about our real plans," warned Daedalus. "Don't even say that you'll be gone for a long time."

"I understand, Father. No one will know that part."

Daedalus Rising

Chapter 17

The Abyss

We have not even to risk the adventure alone, For the heroes of all time have gone before us. The labyrinth is thoroughly known. We have only to follow the thread of the hero path and where we had thought to find an abomination, we shall find a god. And where we had thought to slay another, we shall slay ourselves. Where we had thought to travel outward, we will come to the center of our own existence. And where we had thought to be alone, we will be with all the world.

~Joseph Campbell, The Power of Myth

The next night while Icarus slept, Daedalus carried out the unfinished task, his final act in the restoration work on the palace. If it was to be done at all, he had to do it alone. Taking a long spool of very fine thread, he made his way back to the opening of a tunnel that one of his crews had dug out some years before.

In rebuilding the palace, one of first tasks they had faced was restoring and renovating the labyrinth. In the days following the earthquake and the collapse of walls and caving in of roofs, a good rain turned the palace into a giant funnel, collecting and channeling water downward, into the low places. Some of it would evaporate. Some would be collected by slaves into urns or anything else that would hold water and passed along a human chain toward the closest outside wall and dumped. Most of the rain water, however, would flow inexorably down into the deepest depths of the palace. The labyrinth became a virtual underground lake. The once clear rainwater turned stagnant and foul smelling, home to the dark and secretive creatures that tend to dwell in such places.

To drain the water away, or at least some of it, Daedalus decided on a location in the earth below the palace, that provided the shortest distance for digging a tunnel up and into the hidden maze. For many weeks, the crew dug and drilled upward into the side of the hill, boring and chiseling a tunnel with shovels and hammers and iron rods, until they finally broke through into the labyrinth from below. For a few brief minutes, there was an exuberant gush of cascading black water, rocks and bottom dwelling things. It rushed out in a torrent, finally free of its earthen confines and surging with wild abandon in its effort to rejoin the bluer Mediterranean waters.

When the flow ebbed, Daedalus and his crew entered the labyrinth from below. Even with torches and each other's company, it was still a fearful place. He could still remember the grip of fear, the anxiety that he felt as he entered the dark and damp stillness of that place. There were just too many unpleasant stories about it. That same day, another team of workers entered the labyrinth from the palace above. His team traveled upward from the tunnel they had made, through the twisting passages; both teams calling out, talking loudly, staying close, doing the kinds of things that men do in groups to hide their fear and celebrating well when they finally met. Daedalus made a rudimentary map and later the lower tunnel entrance was sealed.

At least, it had been until tonight. Daedalus was now returning alone to that old unused entrance. With an iron bar and some serious leverage, he removed the rocks that barred the entrance to the forgotten tunnel. Then, tying off one end of the fine thread to a large rock, he began his trek through the labyrinth, alone this time and with nothing but a single torch. He didn't know whether there were prisoners within it or not. If there were, he just hoped they would be more interested in finding a way out than in interfering with him. That made some sense, but still his breathing was shallow and the old fear returned. This time there was no one to look to for support. This time, all he could do was keep moving. It was the fear of the unknown, of anything and everything that lay beyond the circle of light that he held in his hand. Through the fear, he had asked himself again and again, why he was doing this thing. There was no simple answer.

Partly he felt responsible for the fate of the next group of young Athenian slaves that were coming to the island. Without his efforts, Minos would not possess such a readily accessible and effective tool for their torment. The idea of helping them by marking a passage way out of the prison gave him hope, a useful thing for overcoming the fear. He might save some lives if the plan worked. It wasn't a need to challenge or defy the king that drove him that night. Daedalus recognized that over the years, Minos had been very good to him and to Icarus. He just didn't want anyone else to lose their life in a structure he had helped to construct.

Each step onward was like taking back a piece of it. He moved as quickly as he could through the dark confining passages, finally making his way to the stout door that marked the entrance to the palace and the world above. The portal was locked from the other side.

"With the king on the other side, I am safer down here," he thought to himself with a smile.

Looking about the entryway, Daedalus searched until he found just the right place to tie off the other end of the thread. Just beyond the hinge of the door, a large angular rock protruded out into the passageway. It was high enough that someone who had just been locked inside might find it, groping desperately in the darkness. It was perfect, just enough so that the next prisoner of Minos, if they were clever enough and lucky, they might find that thread. And if they kept their wits and followed it, they might find their way out. But that is another story.

With a sigh Daedalus reversed his steps and headed back into the dark passageways. He moved more quickly now,

The True Story of Icarus

following the thread back the way he had come, until he found that place where the string passed downward into the tunnel which he and his crew had constructed a few years before. The shadowy, wet passages of the labyrinth continued in other directions.

Shaking his head as if to say never again, Daedalus turned toward the tunnel and eased himself feet first into its narrow embrace, passing through its confines for the last time. He knew that with this act he was severing whatever remained of his relationship with Minos. It was a decision that was months in the making, to regain control of his own future and to provide Icarus that same opportunity.

At the end of the tunnel, Daedalus was greeted by the starry splendor of the night sky, viewed from a remote place. After the narrow confinement of the labyrinth, the warm earth beneath his feet was a blessing. He stopped and breathed in the night air. It was so immense and beautiful. He could feel his own life surging within him, full and complete, as if it were bursting against the insides of his skin. He raised his arms, palms upward, in appreciation. For a brief moment an energetic connection surged through him, seeming to come up out of the earth and into his spine like a living connection between the earth and the stars.

He spoke his name into the night, quietly at first. Hearing no reply, he said it again, the second time louder, with passion and purpose. He dropped his arms and stood in silence for a moment longer. After a few more moments, he began walking back to the apartment, the home that he knew so well, feeling very alive.

Chapter 18

The Quest

*The adventure that the hero gets
is the one that he is ready for.*
~Joseph Campbell, The Power of Myth

It was a long mountainous island surrounded by boundless beaches and rocky cliffs, separating the land from the warm, blue waters of the Mediterranean. In the summer months, the sun always seemed to shine and where there was the right combination of water and soil, the vegetation lush. Tiny settlements dotted the coasts, small communities in close connection with the sea and the land. In their journey together, Icarus and Daedalus walked along much of the island's outer edge, moving from one village to the next, never staying long in one place. Looking for, but never quite finding the right person with the right boat, to take them off of the island. Several months passed in this way and their journey has nearly circumscribed the island, skirting the rocky, snow covered peaks that dominated the island's core.

As the summer waned, they trekked along the island's western shore. High in the wall of a gorge that emptied into the sea, they found a large cave protected from the prevailing wind. From the cave, a game trail lead up to a high cliff that offered a commanding view of the rocky shore and a beautiful expanse of sky layered upon a clear blue sparkling sea. It was a place of great beauty and there was fresh water, nearby citrus and olive trees, abundant native birds and animals and access to the sea.

After resting there for several days, Daedalus suggested that they stay in this place until the rainy months passed. The nearest village was many miles behind them and the cave had no sign of habitation by others. The bounty of the land and sea would sustain them and its isolation would protect them from the eyes and the reach of the king, he reasoned.

Icarus on the other hand, had just left one home. It was too soon for him to be deciding on another. He liked to stand on the rocky prominence, high above the sea and look out toward the edges of the water and the sky, feeling the irrepressible attraction for the distant places and all the things that he had yet to see and feel. To his eyes, there was excitement and adventure just beyond the wavy haze of the grey blue horizon and his youthful heart was full of an eagerness and anticipation to see more of it. The sky merged into the blue sea all around him and from his vantage point, he knew intuitively that better things awaited him.

Daedalus too, enjoyed the view from the rock. There was a comfortable place along its contours to spread out a sleeping skin and he could spend hours there, gazing across the sea to the north, towards Athens. It was different for Daedalus. He was not heeding adventure's call. There was instead, a pulling at the heart, an undeniable attraction that he imagined was his ancestors, calling him back to his boyhood home.

Since leaving the palace, most of their nights were spent in the open air. Their senses were heightened, more attuned to the animals and birds and to the natural elements that now shaped their days. It was a time of connection, to the earth and to each other. The two rose with the sun, nourished themselves from the bounty of the land or the sea and slept when the earth became dark. It was the sun imposing its constant rhythm on their lives, a slow, steady, ancient heartbeat.

Sitting on his place high above the water, Daedalus enjoyed watching the birds that lived along the cliffs. There was a large colony of darting white and brown ones just a short distance away. During the daylight there was constant motion; birds swooping down from their nests on the ledges to the sea in a never ending search for feeder fish. With some difficulty, he began picking out individual nests and the birds that occupied them, learning their ways. For countless hours, he watched them dive down from above and glide out over the water on outstretched wings. Then the wings would raise up, stalling the glide and with short legs extended the webbed feet entered the water, splashing, wings outstretched, finding a new balance and paddling away, buoyant and searching once more for food.

There were many kinds of birds and Daedalus watched them all. He was fascinated with the way the large ones could use the wind and the air currents to ride upward into the sky, circling higher and higher and then soar, gliding effortlessly, wings outstretched.

"Interesting," he thought, "that the large soaring birds seemed to prefer a solitary existence." It was rare to see two of them together in the sky, sharing the same high altitudes.

"They have such agility and grace," he thought. "Perhaps they become so absorbed by the experience of it that they just don't care that much about each other's company."

Countless birds made their homes along the shore. Huge flocks of small ones filled the sky with their darting bodies and shrieking sounds whenever a predator approached. Mostly the predators were other birds, eagles and hawks. They could sometimes take a smaller bird right out of the air and one of them swooping in was a source of great drama and excitement to the colony.

The best to watch were the soaring birds, the albatross and the condor. They could soar endlessly, gliding majestically on the winds and without effort. With white undersides blended into the sky, the albatross were difficult to spot at a distance. The condors, with their large black bodies and larger wingspans were easier on the eyes. Even in the higher altitudes they seemed to dwarf the other birds. After returning to Athens, finding a

The True Story of Icarus

condor's nest among the rocky crags of the island was Daedelus' next favorite daydream. He longed to watch them take off into the air and land, see how they lived and see, close up, just how large the birds actually were.

Icarus rarely joined in the birdwatching. He could not sit for long. He had to be moving, doing. There was so much energy in him. It seemed to flow out of him with every motion. His days were spent hunting and fishing and exploring the island and he took great pride in supplying most of their food. He quickly learned every game trail, every tidal pool and every source of fresh water for miles around. He could scramble up and down the rocky trails between the sea and the land all day long, never seeming to tire and with the skill and agility of one of the island goats.

One day, Daedalus began collecting feathers. He made his way to the nearby ledges of the sea bird colonies and started with the easy to find, small, fluffy ones. In no time at all, he had gathered a great pile of them and then he and Icarus each had a pillow for their heads at night.

Extending his search, it was not long before he found a single, long dark feather. He wanted to believe that it was from one of the condors. Sometimes, he found feathers with colorful hues in elegant designs. Other times, he was drawn to their unusual shape, or size. Many of them he saved in a safe dry place inside the cave. Then he expanded his search again, finding more nesting places in different directions, again and again, collecting feathers of all sizes and shapes.

After a time, the inside of the cave became covered in piles of feathers, sorted by size and shape. Sometimes Daedalus made designs out of them, then the designs become wall hangings, or mobiles that hung for a time on the inside of the cave. Then Icarus began to join him in the search for more feathers, especially the long ones, from the tails of the large predator birds. They both appreciated the beauty of these powerful birds in flight and the long sweeping curve of the feathers that comprised the wings that held them aloft.

Daedalus Rising

Pensively gazing out across the sea one day, while holding the quill of a long black feather in one hand and stroking it between the thumb and forefinger of the other, Daedalus remembered his last conversation with King Minos. He remembered how the king had responded to his challenge, the anger that ensued and the king taking control with his threats and intimidation. He could still hear the words.

"That you master builder, can no sooner leave the island than you can fly."

He wondered whether they intended to mock and degrade, or was that only his own perception? Weeks later, alone on the cliff, he responded again, "Well, thank you King Minos for the idea, a completely wild and inspired idea. Why just make models and wall hangings out of the feathers? Why not make wings? Wings to fly off the island! Escape from Minos!"

That very day inside the cave, Daedalus began arranging the feathers according to size and strength. From studying the soaring birds he knew that a proper wingspan would have to be at least twice his own height and he began considering different woods and how to construct the right frame. He experimented with ways to bind or braid the feathers together and by the evening an intricate network of feathers lay on the floor of the cave, with a gentle curving outer arc.

Carrying several fish for their dinner, Icarus returned to the cave that night and saw that his father was building wings, big ones, big enough for a man's shoulders. Daedalus did not hear him approach. He was concentrating, focused on his handiwork. Icarus stopped and watched for a long time without words. Then he laughed, broke the silence and asked, "So this is the plan for leaving the island?"

Daedalus looked up and smiled in response. He was excited and happy, his words flowing in a steady torrent. Yes, he had a plan. A plan to make wings that would hold a man on the currents of air, wings to use to fly off the island. No, not really flying. More like soaring, gliding on the currents of air like the condors did. Daedalus grew more and more animated as he talked, completely lost in the energy and beauty of his dream.

Icarus didn't interrupt. He has seen his father become absorbed in projects before. He has seen the focus and the drive and he knew that his father could get carried away with an idea and then devote hours and hours to developing it. Sometimes, after much work and detail, he'd created an impressive result. He has seen it happen before in his father's work with buildings of wood and stone.

"You know Icarus, I have been dreaming of flying for a long time. What if it just came down to matters of equipment and technique? Would you try it?"

Icarus just smiled.

When Daedalus got carried away with an idea, he could be very enthusiastic, especially at first. His energy would just overflow and often times, people were drawn to the power of the idea. Icarus saw it happen, the contagion of the enthusiasm and he had no intention of hindering the flow. If nothing else, it was sure to be entertaining and he wanted to hear what his father had to say. Besides, who wouldn't want to soar like an eagle, he wondered? Icarus closed his eyes and listened to the words, imagining himself free to go in any direction that he chose.

"Does an eagle select its own direction?" he asked out loud, "Or does it just wait for wind to choose its course?"

Daedalus didn't respond but instead dropped the framework of feathers onto the floor of the cave, threw up his arms and exclaimed, "This will never work. I've got more feathers than I can count, but there is nothing to bind them together in a strong enough network. That's the biggest problem. We need an adhesive, strong enough to hold the weight of a man. All we have is this insipid candle wax." Daedalus shook his fists in mock frustration. "Wax is so brittle it wouldn't provide enough support to hold up a wet dog." Dropping his hands in mock defeat he concluded, "There has to be something better we can use."

Daedalus was about to propose that they leave their home in the cave by the sea and begin a search for the right glue, traveling together, the way they always had. Icarus, who was mostly silent since entering the cave spoke up, before his father could say another word and interjected, "Maybe I can find something that will work."

Daedalus looked at him quizzically, saying nothing.

"I'm getting bored just hanging around here all day, every day. It is truly a beautiful place. All the sun and sea I can handle. But we're all alone out here."

Dismayed, Daedalus turned to his son and looked at him, a bittersweet moment. The boy that he was so used to interacting with was not there. Instead, he saw looking back at another man: a willful and strong young man with incredible endurance. Someone who could live off the land as easily as a wild goat.

It was Icarus, not him, not the father, that provided their food since settling into this home near the cliff by the sea. Every passing day, he let Icarus take over more and more of the responsibility for their lives. Icarus was good at it and it was easy to increasingly rely on him. In a flash of understanding, Daedalus saw that Icarus was aware of this shift. This was surely the secret for making the better person, thought Daedalus, to grow in the open air and to eat and sleep with the earth.

In one way, they were their own family, a community of two. Icarus wanting to go now, to leave, threatened to break that unity apart. That part hurt. But Daedalus also heard a deeper message, that Icarus wanted to keep the connection, but in a different way. He was clearly seeking independence, but at the same time still wanting to assist in order to reach for the improbable goal of winged flight. And the motivation had all originated within Icarus. It was completely voluntary and from a willing spirit. Icarus wanted to take on the risks and the adventure of journeying alone into the unknown places of the island, with his father's purpose as a guide. That thought resonated for Daedalus and he was more than pleased.

The True Story of Icarus

Daedalus could also see the parallels between what was happening between himself and Icarus, and his own departure from the service of the king. He had modeled the very same kind of change just a few months before. Now Icarus told him in his own way, that it was time for him to step into his own journey. How fortunate could he be? Just a few minutes before he had been ranting about having no adhesive for the wings. Now his son was offering to make that search his quest. This was all happening in exactly the right order, the right time and place for them both. All Daedalus had to do was let him go and get out of the way, but that would not be an easy thing to do.

Tears came to his eyes and Daedalus realized that he had to make a lasting memory out of this, commemorate it for the milestone that it was. Finding his voice, Daedalus told Icarus that his plan was a good one. That it was time and that it was right for Icarus to go on this part of the journey alone.

"If I went along, I would only slow you down," Daedalus told him. And then with a gleam in his eye he said, "I am very proud of you right now. This is your challenge, your quest and no one else on the entire planet is better suited to this than you."

He paused for a minute and thought to himself, trying to remember his own time of departure from family, "What did I want to hear from my father?"

Thinking back on this time in his own youth, he had no memory of any words from his father and certainly, no memory of an initiation. He could not remember hearing any kind of blessing and now, he wished for it. He wanted very much to have a memory of some words of recognition, approval and acceptance.

Understanding this, Daedalus stood up and turned to Icarus and motioned for him to rise as well. "And I will bless you now," he said, placing both hands upon his son's shoulders and looked into his eyes. "I bless you your strengths: your courage, your kindness and your judgment. And I honor this quest, knowing that you begin this journey unsure of the destination, yet without uncertainty or doubt. Travel well and return to this place when you are satisfied, with shining eyes, whole and healthy."

Icarus did not reply.

He really didn't understand what it was that his father was getting teary about. He thought that his original suggestion had been perfectly reasonable and rather obvious, at that.

They built a small fire on the lee side of a rock wall, cooked the dinner that Icarus provided and talked late into the night. It was a hopeful time, full of laughter and ideas about what might lie ahead.

Daedalus had plenty of worries about Icarus journeying alone, but he kept most of them to himself. There was always the possibility that they might never see each other again. Anything could happen. Icarus could become injured somehow; a fall, a broken bone or a deep cut. So many things could go wrong, so many obstacles might get in the way. But those things could just as easily happen here by the cave. For that matter, Daedalus might be the one to get hurt. None of these fears constituted a reason not to go forward. The only true course was to move ahead with the plan.

There was of course, the issue of King Minos. There might even be a reward for their capture by now. What if Icarus met someone along the way that tried to take advantage of him, in order to gain that reward? Anything could happen out there. That's right, he told himself. Good things could happen, as well as bad. He might just as readily find someone with a stout boat, someone eager to leave the island for his own reasons and ready and willing to take them both anywhere they pleased.

"It must be this way," he told himself. "I'm not going to concentrate on the things that could go wrong. Surely there are many, but no more than the outcomes that are welcome and that is where my thoughts will dwell." Imagining the two of them in flight over the sea, he finally found the peace in which to fall asleep.

Icarus had no difficulty falling asleep that night. It had been a long day and he was tired. He was also relieved and pleased with the outcome. He had not expected his practical father to agree so readily with his idea. Full of youthful exuberance, Icarus was supremely confident of his ability to live on his own, anywhere on the island. As he closed his eyes, his imagination began to run wildly to the places, the animals and even to the people that he might encounter, all on his own, without Daedalus there to act or to speak first. He would explore the island, the faraway beaches, the gorges and the mountaintops with no one to tell him what to do or how to do it.

He would be alert for the glue, the missing ingredient the wings, but more than that, he wanted to learn everything there was to know about the secret places of the island. He felt so fit, so vital, so full of life. Whatever lay ahead, it would be a magnificent adventure. And while Daedalus dreamt of winged flight, Icarus saw himself standing on a mountaintop at the center of the island, staring out in every direction. Each in his own way, had an entire island below his feet.

The next morning, father and son shared a breakfast of olives and oranges from the trees in the nearly hills. Few words were spoken. Daedalus tried to think of a way to tell his son to keep himself safe and not to stay away too long. Icarus was simply eager to go and felt as if everything that needed to be said, had been said the night before.

Finally, Daedalus smiled and told his son that he himself, was not going anywhere. He would live there by the cave and study the birds, the condor and the albatross and learn how they soared so effortlessly. There was much to do. He would find their nests and watch and learn how it was that they take off and land. And he would find a way to make a lightweight frame for wings with a proper wingspan, large enough to hold a man. And he would be there waiting near the cliff by the sea when Icarus returned.

"And we will have a feast and a wonderful celebration. I promise you." With tears stinging the corners of his eyes, he told his son that it was important that he make rich and wonderful memories, so that when he returned they would have good stories to share around the fire."

Daedalus Rising

"What about the glue?" asked Icarus.

"That too," replied his father.

Icarus grinned back at him. He tried to assure his father that there was nothing to worry about. That he would return soon, as soon as he finished the quest. He looked into his father's caring face and promised that he would either have the right glue with him when he returned, or know where to find it.

And then once the right amount of tears were shed and the last hug exchanged, Icarus turned and left his father standing on the rocky promontory that overlooked the sea. He carried his sleeping skin, his bow, a knife, a fishing line, some dried food, a water bladder and his father's blessing.

Chapter 19

Return To The Dreamtime

*The great Western truth is that each one of us
is a completely unique creature and that,
if we are ever to give any gift to the world,
it will have to come out of our own experience
and the fulfillment of our own potentialities.*
~Joseph Campbell, The Power of Myth

Sitting by a small cooking fire, Daedalus dined on fresh sea bass and watched another sun drop into the sea in a panorama of orange and pink and blue. The coals of the fire glowed in the light breeze that washed fresh salt air over his face. It was so serene that evening, the sense of being in just the right place and time. Evenings like this were good ones. To have all this beauty around him was well worth whatever hardship came with being alone. He had not slept on a bed in months and did not miss it. That was just a part of his growing sense of connection to the earth and its rhythms.

Tonight was the return of the new moon, a darkness that marked the beginning of its cycle of transformation into fullness and completion and then back again. The moon had its own distinctive rhythm, so different from the constant daily beat of the sun. The lunar cycle spoke of growth and renewal, of becoming whole and complete from nothing and then returning back to nothing.

Daedalus Rising

Standing up he walked to the edge of the cliff and hung his toes over the edge. "That could be my life right now," he mused, "So little form or substance, I seem to have detached myself from everything I once thought of as important. It is all potential now."

He held out his arms into the gentle wind blowing onto his chest. "Here I am," he said and he leaned forward as far as he dared into the wind closing his eyes. He imagined what he could do with long beautiful wings attached at his shoulders. "Here, I am," he thought and then laughed to himself as he spoke to the wind, "Once a builder of earth and wood and stone. Now I am a builder of wings."

He looked out across the water, a warm glow in his chest. It was the right conclusion for the day, a moment of pure spontaneity and reflection. Looking briefly out to sea again he took a few slow deep breaths and returned to the place near the rock where his sleeping skin lay on the soft earth.

It would be a dark, starry night, if the clouds stayed away. He felt tired. Sleep should come easily tonight, he thought with a smile. Finding just the right sandy spot, he lay down, his eyes open, reflecting on the day. He thought about Icarus and he wondered where he would be laying his head tonight. Somewhere warm and dry, he hoped. He thought about what he wanted for Icarus and he imagined him, smiling and happy. Daedalus put that image in his head and kept it there. As he turned onto his back, his attention turned to a few of the brighter stars just beginning to make their appearance. His eyes closed and sleep took hold of him.

Later that night, the flight dream returned.

In the dreamtime, Daedalus walked back on the same empty green field, the lush fertile place, surrounded by gently rolling hills. He was barefoot and his eyes were closed. He began to feel a tingling in his knees and a vibration which rose up from the soft ground through his feet, legs, hips and into his chest. Then there was a slight breeze and he turned his body into it, until he could feel the wind full upon his face. The wind picked up. It lifted his arms without any effort, the breeze flowed against his chest. The force of it increased a little more. It blew into him, through him. The energy of the wind resonated in his chest, joining and mixing in powerful harmony with the vibration that was surging upwards, through his torso. Then the engaging energy of the sun enveloped him and pulled at his chest.

This time, he knew the uplift was coming. He still remembered the sensation, even though it had been years since he had felt its power. He could feel it coming and this time, he decided, he was not going to wait for it. There was no need to wait. It was almost there, almost time. He could feel the inevitability of its approach. Like a long awaited climax, there was a powerful surge that could not be suppressed, could not be kept in. Anticipating the lift, he eagerly dropped his weight into his knees and then pushed himself upward, extending his legs, twisting and throwing his body up into the air as high and as far as he could lift himself, arms outstretched, beaming, trusting that the currents of air would catch him and hold him. And they did.

In the morning, Daedalus awoke with a vitality that would not be contained. The energy of the dream filled him up. It was a song in his heart that filled his lungs and every pore in his body. He walked, he bounced and leapt onto the path that led around the cliff face and down to the sea, where he swam and bathed.

Sitting on his rumpled clothes next to the water, the early morning sun dried his skin. He looked up into the silent sky and saw the dark silhouette of a large soaring bird. There were white markings under broad black wings, long wings at least twice the length of the body. He stared, silently watching the graceful, effortless motion of the bird as it sailed through the air. "It is so big," he wondered to himself, "how can such a huge bird soar through the air with so much grace and so little effort?"

With that question and more filling his thoughts, he reached for his clothes, simultaneously walking and stepping into them, hurrying back to the cliff face and the trail leading up to the camp. He trotted up the path as quickly as his lungs would allow, back to the cave where his few belongings were kept. Grabbing the few things he would need, the bladder that held his fresh water, the fishing line and his sleeping skin, he began to walk briskly, following the flight of the soaring bird, eager to study its ways.

Chapter 20

Icarus' Journey

> *He was alone. He was unheeded, happy and near to the wild heart of life. He was alone and young and willful and wildhearted, alone amid a waste of wild air and brackish waters and the seaharvest of shells and tangle and veiled, grey sunlight.*
>
> ~James Joyce, Ulysses

Icarus walked into a wild, magnificent country. He wandered through huge stretches of green and fertile plains, high plateaus bordered by barren, craggy ridges and snow-capped mountains. Standing on a high precipice one evening, he overlooked a narrow gorge, hundreds of meters deep. He watched in amazement as a raging torrent of water filled the cobbled floor, carrying trees and boulders and anything else that was lying about, fueled by a nearby cloudburst of rain.

It was nature, beautiful and pure and elemental. With each day that he journeyed through the island's courses, the deeper he immersed himself. It was the realization of boyhood dreams, dreams about wandering across the rocky wastelands of the island, scrambling up the ledges of cliffs, climbing the mountains and descending rock walled gorges until he came to the sea and searched for the perfect place to swim or to fish. He was living his dreams now. Since he had walked away from the home he shared with his father by the sea and into the wild, these boyhood dreams had become his daily life.

He took on greater and greater challenges, testing the limits of his endurance and his will. In his earlier adventures with

Daedalus around the island, they walked and climbed and camped in many wonderful places. Looking back on all those times, it was as if he was preparing for this all along. It was what his spirit longed for. A lone wanderer, the days filled themselves easily with passion and intensity. On the most memorable of them, he heedlessly strained and punished his body in ways that would probably not have occurred to him, had his father been nearby. Imagining him wandering alone along the rocky cliffs by the sea, it occurred to Icarus that no one else had ever aroused in him such a hunger to please. No one else had ever instilled so much corked fury.

With the passing days, he thought less and less about either the future or the past. The necessities of finding the food and the water sustained him. These practicalities, for the most part, kept him fully occupied in the present. There wasn't that much opportunity for reflection, at least not until the sun went down. Sometimes at night, he commemorated the adventure of the day with his own high invocation, howling his song into the moonlight and the stars and into the teeth of the world. He became a part of the natural beauty of the island.

Three mountain peaks lay along an east west line across the center of the island. The paths that Icarus followed drew him inexorably toward the middle one in the very center of the island. The high ridges were like a magnet, pulling on him with an irresistible force. As he tramped across the high plateau, drawn by the high peaks in the distance, he replenished himself from the olive and citrus trees that flourished in the fertile soils and from the meat of the wild goats that roamed heedlessly across the plains.

He knew as well that soon he would leave behind the fertile plateaus and the way would become rocky and steep. For much of it he would have only the food and water that he could carry. He had gone without before. And more than that, he carried an overriding and sometimes reckless belief in his own destiny; he knew that eventually there would be water. After all, it was a snow covered peak.

This journey would take however long it needed. Crossing the high plateau and making his approach were all in the willful pursuit of the same dream. He found both stimulation and fulfillment. It was a calling within himself.

That night he camped by a grove of cyprus trees, the last he would see for awhile. He was on the flank of the mountain and above him the vegetation grew short and sparse and then would be gone. In the morning he would be traversing across the rocky slopes. He thought of the words that his father had told him, all those times at the end of the day when he was a boy, that there was no one quite like him in the whole world and he could do anything, go anywhere, be anything, that he wanted. That night he replayed many memories of their times together. It was so good to be alive; to be living under the deep blue sky with the delightful experiences that each day brought. None of it would have been possible if Daedalus had not brought him to this island all those years ago. "When I do get back there," Icarus said to himself, "I must tell him how grateful I am for everything that we did together. He was the one who brought me to this island. I must remember to tell him that."

The next morning, he began his climb. Since beginning his trek upon the island interior, he had lost weight. His body was leaner and harder than it had been in the days back in the palace. It wasn't so much physical strength but vitality, he was sure of himself and his abilities. There was a confidence growing in him like he had never known before. He moved steadily upward over the rocky ground, traversing the slope in a measured pace.

He thought about all the changes that occurred since leaving the palace. There really was no reason to go back. Daedalus was right about that part, but they were so very different, he and his father. Icarus was sure of that. His father wanted to leave the island and to travel to other places. Icarus had come to understand that what he wanted, what he longed for, was to live in the wilds of this one. One day, he'd tell his father that as well.

The island was huge and there were so many beautiful places to see. He knew that he would go back to the cave by the sea

Daedalus Rising

someday; maybe in the spring or summer. For now he was having too good a time to even consider it. That was his father's home and more and more, he understood that he was separated from it. He knew that Daedalus expected him and was waiting for him to return and knew that he would, but it would not be the same.

When he did return he would persuade Daedalus that there was no real need to leave the island. If Minos searched for them at all, it would be on the water. And the search would not begin until the king realized that they were not returning. He would expect them to flee by boat for another island and not even consider following them into the island's interior, into the wilds. They could easily evade anyone that might try to pursue them. There were so many gorges and hidden places. They would be safe right here. Of course, staying on the island meant that there would be no need for the adhesive and no crazy dream of flying. That was his father's dream and it seemed to have become a mission, but it was not Icarus'.

"How easy would it be for him to let it go?" Icarus wondered aloud.

He thought about these things and more as he hiked to the lower saddle and then followed the ridge line along its length, until reaching the next and the next, gradually making his way up the slope. After several hours of walking, he paused to enjoy the view. He was high enough to see the water on both sides, getting a glimpse of just how narrow a strip of land it really was. And he was high enough to spot a soaring bird from above. This one stayed in his view for a long time, gliding on the winds. He would remember to tell Daedalus about it someday.

There was quite a lot to see from this vantage point. There were times to keep track of his footing, but mostly he wanted to keep his eyes on the way that lay ahead, scouting the distance to reach the next ridge and the one after that. At times he would scan the horizon and blue sea that encircled the island and him in the middle of it all. This journey was a matter of one step following the next and the will to keep going. He moved higher and clouds enveloped him in grey mist. Sometimes they parted and there was a glimpse of the way, but mostly he just had to move forward, believing that the peak was still ahead.

When he reached the point where the ground leveled off, there was nowhere any higher to go. Grey sky was all around and he stood on a gently sloping patch of snow, broken by large angular rocks. Sweat and warm sun filled his face. He drank and caught his breath in a silent celebration. More sky than land, it was a surreal place that did not engender loitering.

The sun that warmed his face broke apart the billowy thickness of the clouds. Little by little, they thinned and revealed the entire island, as if it were a map laid out under his feet. There were the brown arcs of the sandy beaches, separating the blue and the grey sea from the land. The sea never seemed to end. It was there in every direction, the same grey merging of water and sky, repeated over and over wherever he looked. These were the boundaries of his world, but like Daedalus he understood that there was more, much more.

Daedalus Rising

Chapter 21

Soaring Lessons

Our deepest fear is not that we are inadequate. Our deepest fear is that we are powerful beyond measure. It is our light which we fear most, not our darkness.

~Marianne Williamson

The flight dream had returned and with it an exhilaration that energized his own longing for flight. With a steady pace, he followed behind the large soaring black bird, trying as best he could to keep it in view. It stayed aloft for hours. Could it possibly be searching all this time, or was it just choosing the sky, preferring to soar rather than to perch upon a motionless earth. It was visible from so far away, the dark undersides of the body a silhouette against the sky. White patches under each wing marked it as the one to follow. Daedalus watched and walked and slowly made his way across the rocky landscape, moving northward and paralleling the coastline.

The bird maneuvered with so little exertion, so little movement. Down below Daedalus was in constant motion and effort to keep the bird in view. He would almost catch up, only to fall behind again, time after time. Finally, he was able to gain some ground when the bird found a column of warm rising air and effortlessly rode it upwards. Daedalus dripped sweat on the warm earth, following and watching. And then, as if it had grown impatient with waiting for him to catch up, the bird banked its long wings and without even a discernable movement, left the thermal and moved rapidly across the sky, away from the man below.

"Where was that bird going?" he wondered. "How much further can it be from its home?" As best Daedalus could tell, its feet were clawed and not webbed. So there had to be a nest somewhere on the island. Eventually, it had to land. He would be close by when it did. When he found that place, he would find the best spot to observe and study its ways. He hoped that there would be more than one. Most of all, he wanted to see how such a large bird frees itself from gravity's grip. If he could just get close enough to see the spreading of the wings and the taking of flight, then it would all be worthwhile.

All day long, the bird stayed aloft. The man patiently followed, back and forth across the landscape, taking a parallel path with the bird overhead. Until late in the afternoon, when the soaring black bird slightly pulled in its wings and went into a steady descent. Daedalus broke into a trot, hurrying to keep it in view. He had walked many miles that day and would not be able to keep up his pace for long, but it wasn't yet time to rest. He had to keep going.

The bird descended towards a rocky place high above a strip of rocky beach. Daedalus was close enough to see it drop below the side of a high cliff, the wings flexing back to push against the air, as it dropped its body into some hidden place along the rock wall. Far away on the flat higher ground, Daedalus stood and watched, catching his breath and congratulating himself for having come this far. Nothing to do now except to find out where the nest was. He found a protected place to spend the night and tend to his own needs.

From all the day's exertion, he was very tired and he fell asleep with visions of the soaring bird in his head, retracing his steps from the day. While he slept, the flight dream returned. He was no longer on the green field. Instead, he stood in the sunlight on a thin strip of rocky beach, next to a high cliff wall. His breathing was relaxed and deep and the warmth of the sun was a glow upon his chest. The muscles around his sternum enlarged and tightened as if large wings enveloped his shoulders as he flexed and relaxed them in the morning sun. Energy poured into his body through the sun, filling him and lifting him by his chest and into the sky. It freed him from the earth.

Spiraling upward, he passed long vertical fractures in the rock wall and the sound of the surf below grew dim. As he passed the top of the rocky ledge, trees and bluffs and rolling hills came into view. He was met by the wind. The sounds and smells of the sea receded and he rose higher, moving up above the landscape. Rocks and trees that once stood before his eyes, blurred and then shrank, receding into the distance. He rose still higher and the wind increased. The edge of the rocky bluff became a fine line separating blue sea from brown earth. Viewed from the sky, the earth transitioned from a collection of individual rocks and trees, into a flat patchwork of textures and colors.

Now the wind was very strong. He turned his body into it and felt it push against his chest and roar past his ears. The force of it pushed him upwards and back, driving him higher into the sky, in much the same way that the soaring bird had moved earlier that day. It was a delicate balance to keep his chest into the wind, shifting and moving ever so slightly with just the right pitch to let the wind lift him higher and not push him backwards.

High above the island, he spied a protected bay and turned his head and then the shoulders in its direction, banking his body and letting the wind bring him around. Completing the turn and lower now, he found himself in a river of wind, deep and wide, coming from behind. He was soaring and he thought that if he could always be in the sky that way, then he might never tire of wandering. He understood now how a great soaring bird might choose to live in solitude.

The wind made no sound when he traveled with it and it pushed him onward toward the bay, through a gradual descent into the pull of the earth's attraction. His skills in the air were increasing. The first few times that he flew in the dreamtime, he was roughly pushed about wherever the winds and the opposing gravities conspired to take him. And he was thrilled with it, to

The True Story of Icarus

feel the currents of air washing over him. In the early times, he was happy just to be in the sky, graceless and awkward and with no direction of his own. On those first times in the sky, he was a gangly intruder, like a drunken man stumbling about in an earthquake.

Tonight was different. He realized that there was more to flying than just being blown about by forces greater than him. For the first time, he had chosen his own destination and now he was heading for it, a small beautiful bay sparkling in the moonlight. There was definitely a technique to flight and as he put more of himself into it, he began to feel the confidence that he could go where he wanted to go. So he paid more attention to the maneuvering of his body, what worked and what didn't. He just spent an entire day watching one bird soar. If only he could have that kind grace and agility in the sky.

So he began his lessons, twisting, stretching and turning his body to test the equilibrium and still maintain his stability. It took all of his effort and concentration to constantly shift his balance in response to changing fields and air currents. It was like learning to walk all over again. There were times when he found just the right balance and for a moment, it became effortless. Then he got distracted, or tired or a change in the wind caught him off guard. Then he tumbled along the energy gradient until with enough struggle and squirming, he found his direction once again.

For many days, Daedalus stayed near the nesting ground and watched and learned all that he could. He soon discovered where the nest was hidden, high up on a ledge overlooking the sea, but not so high that it was approachable from above. He found his own vantage points and soon learned that there were actually three birds, all of them very large. Two had the white markings on the undersides of the wings, but the third was all black. Daedalus guessed that it must be a young chick, waiting to come into its first molting and the offspring of this mature breeding pair. With recognition made easier because of the

Daedalus Rising

distinctive all black markings, it was the first one to receive a name and Daedalus called it Basia.

Each one of them, even Basia had an incredible wing span, much longer than their bodies. He studied them for days, watching their take offs and landings. He always admired their agility and grace in the sky. And at night, he made his own flights, dreaming the flight dream and soaring in the winds.

Chapter 22

Down From the Mountain

> *An extended stay in the wilderness inevitably directs one's attention outward as much as inward and it is impossible to live off the land without developing both a subtle understanding of and a strong emotional bond with that land and all it holds.*
>
> ~Jon Krakauer, Into the Wild

Standing in the mid-day sun on the top of the snow covered peak, Icarus felt a bit like an outsider, who had wandered into the home of a god. It was a numinous time and place for him, the culmination of an adventure of heedless intensity through the wilds of the island. Much more than just the satisfaction of reaching a day's goal, this was like following an omen, the process of bringing peace to an agitated part of his soul.

In the sun's warmth on the summit, he was perched above the rest of the island. Snowy slopes fell away on all sides, gradually giving way to barren ridges in rocky grey and brown. Fingers of green cut through the rocky terraces, widening into broad fertile plateaus in the lower elevations. Beyond that, the verdant landscape gave way to the sea. It was a spectacular sight and he scanned the view in every direction, taking it all in. The entire world was laid out before him.

In these moments, he gave no thought to Daedalus living by the water's edge, or to Minos in his palace, or to anyone else. In the solitude of the place, he perceived only the physical space he inhabited and the inner man. He felt a sense of overwhelming acceptance, belonging and gratitude. In that moment, there was no other time, no other place to be. All his days of trekking were compressed into that moment of peaceful celebration. He was relieved and satisfied. A huge amount of energy and effort had been poured into this moment and this outcome. The steady wind blew onto his face. It was a constant stream of energy, a force against his chest. There was another stream, a more subtle flow, coming up into his hide-covered feet through the rocks and snow and holding held him fast to the spot. He waited there a while longer, not wanting the sensations to end.

Icarus looked down across the land that sloped away from him in every direction, across the brown and grey rocky slopes to the high green plateaus and the gorges that cut through them. He scanned the landscape in every direction and saw one particular gorge which seemed to stand out from all the rest. Its brown and grey sides bled into darker shades as it grew wider, the hues merged into a deepening green, all of it portending fertility in the opening of the valley into the sea. From the depth of the colors, there must be flowing water in that valley, at least most of the year.

Fresh water was everything in terms of sustaining life. It meant edible plants and wild game and perhaps even people. It had been too long a time since he had talked to anyone and he missed it. With that thought, he became aware of his thirst and the hunger in his stomach. It would soon be time to turn away and leave the summit.

He drank the last of the water from the water bladder and followed it with some of the dried fish and fruit which had sustained him in this climb. While he ate, his gaze returned to the lush green valley. Again, it stood out above all the others. Strange that it could attract his eye above everything else that was arrayed beneath his feet. He closed his eyes and tried to relax and think about something else. But when opened his eyes, they returned to the valley again.

The True Story of Icarus

It occurred to Icarus to do something that would leave a mark upon the summit, some sign that he had passed that way. It was such a unique place, perhaps the highest point of land on the island. He wondered about that, but it is impossible to know. There were many peaks.

To commemorate the day and complete the memory, he built a cairn. There was little to work with, except for the exposed stones below on the windward face. Going back and forth too many times, he was able to turn a few freezing cold rocks into a small conical pyramid. Thinking that his father would certainly appreciate this moment, he said "I am a builder after all," and smiled at the thought.

When it was up to his knees and broad enough for sitting, that was enough for a decent memory. He sat and rested and thought of the colorful gorge as afternoon clouds gathered in around the peaks. When he looked around it was already gone, lost in the milky haze of the clouds. He knew that it was time to leave. Standing, he placed both of his hands on the top of the pyramid and closed his eyes, promising to return one day and sealing the image of the place into his memory. Then he turned and began to descend into the clouds.

He walked quickly across the hardened snow, traversing across the slope until he stopped to take one last look at the pyramid of stones that he left behind, marking the place. Then he made for a protruding ridge of limestone that he followed until it took him out of the snow. In several more hours, he passed through the rocky slopes. Bits of vegetation began to appear. The wind was gone and the air warm once again.

He headed for the gorge that caught his eye from the mountaintop earlier in the day. Hungry but without food, he found a small stone, placed it in his mouth and sucked on it to stimulate the saliva. He could feel the uneven places with his tongue. It kept his tongue and throat moist and he paced himself, breathing through his nose and saving his moisture as he moved across the landscape. By early evening, the head wall of the gorge came into view.

Daedalus Rising

He followed a goat trail across an arid plateau. He hoped it would show him the easiest way to descend through the rocky ledges and into the beginnings of the gorge. Vegetation reappeared, as he dropped down into the stillness of the upper canyon. The air was a little more moist and he could almost smell the sea in it. The floor of the canyon was rocky and covered with smooth rounded stones. Occasional clumps of grass struggled to make their way against the weight of the stones. Walking ahead, the walls of the gorge grew higher and water seeps appeared in the crisscrossing fractures. Sometimes, the seeps supported lush pockets of vines or grass, his own private gardens for a quiet stroll through the evening twilight.

He wanted to find food and a protected spot to spend the night. The gorge had grown in width and the walls were higher still. Occasional pools of water dotted the rocky floor and tadpoles and algae were sometimes visible in the clear, fresh water. The plants grew taller there, occasionally a tamarisk or a pine appeared, usually marking a silent spring. Small channels of flowing water connected the low places. Sometimes there was sand or silt and if often held a record of the animals, the rabbits, the deer and the goats that had gone this way before him. His senses were wide open, fully alert to any sight, sound or smell. He wanted to learn about the other living things that frequented this gorge. Then, he saw something that fixed him in his tracks, unable or unwilling to take another step. He bent down on one knee to the earth and looked more closely at a marking in soft silt. It was the toe print of a human foot.

A gentle breeze blew up the canyon. On it, he heard the soothing sound of falling water and the smell of the sea, and the breeze joined these signs with his own scent and bore them all up the gorge and away. Darkness fell. Torn between his hunger for food, his fatigue and the desire to know more about the maker of the footprint, Icarus paused to consider where he would sleep that night. From the sound of it, he imagined a small pool of water up ahead, backed up against a fallen log and a graceful waterfall at one end. At this time of day, it might also be a popular spot for game and he imagined his next meal coming up the canyon for a drink. He imagined that he might find another hunter already there. Then they would just have to share, he thought with a laugh and then it occurred to him, that the other hunter might already be watching him.

Chapter 23

Daedalus Ascending

The extraordinary occurs in the lives of ordinary people.
~Paulo Coelho, The Alchemist

In the daylight hours, Daedalus gathered the many pieces and parts he would need for the construction of the wings. To carry his own weight aloft, Daedalus understood that he would need much more than just the length of his own two arms. His studies of the proportions of the soaring birds suggested that a wingspan of at least twice the length of the body was necessary. For the wings themselves, he needed the lightest and strongest native wood and a method to attach them to a framework that held them against his own body. There was much to be done.

With Icarus gone now, he relished the evening hours sitting on the rocky prominence between the sea and the sky. For many months, he lived in the outdoors and was very aware of his deepening connection with the earth. His days were no longer defined by schedules or a need to meet deadlines. Instead, he was living within the offsetting rhythms of the sun and moon and the structure they imposed on his days and months.

"I could never have predicted this for myself," he thought, amused by the irony that a builder of palaces and temples would ultimately choose to live under an open sky. There were no more building projects to be completed, at least none subject to another's approval. Now there was only the one, the wings and it was solely his own, something he would share only with Icarus.

These thoughts ran through his head as he announced to no one in particular, "I had to make all these changes, in order to be the man I am becoming." Growing silent again, Daedalus imagined himself in flight over the island, a flying man, a soaring man. Thinking about it now, while wide awake, was little different from the awareness of flight in his dreams. The same sense of vitality and purpose infused both, different perspectives to the same path. Alone now, he could devote all of his energies into creating the wings. It was as if the dream had been guiding him, in some fashion, for all these years and now it was coming together. There seemed to be a wellspring of energy from within that carried him on in the direction of this deepest calling.

It was a time of tremendous change for Icarus as well. Daedalus understood that it was no accident that Icarus had embarked upon his quest, right on the heels of his own breaking away from king Minos. Both of them were emancipating, in their own ways. "And how good a model," he wondered, "have I been?"

Daedalus' thoughts turned to his son. He reminded himself that when Icarus returned, the boy he had known would be gone, replaced by the man. He expected it and supported the changes, whatever that meant. "Even if he comes back empty handed, hungry or hurt. We can deal with any of those things. And if he comes back with all the riches of the king, then we can deal with that too. I must remember, that my role is to make a lasting memory of the return, in the way that I wish my own father might have."

His thoughts reached out to Icarus. He wondered where he was and what he might be doing. His self reliance and independence were a tremendous source of pride for Daedalus. Even though the thought of it had an uncomfortable edge, it was so clear that Icarus demonstrated that he no longer needed or wanted the predictability and safety of his father's promise. He had only to look at the man his son was becoming in order to move past the discomfort brought about by the sense of loss.

Daedalus Rising

It was only his ego, always wanting to be in charge of things that kept getting in the way.

He imagined Icarus moving into his own life and the thought of it brought him a growing sense of satisfaction. Daedalus could just picture him, a vital and energetic young man, here on this island or wherever else he chose, walking or sailing, or flying. Yes, even flying. Icarus was moving on and more than anything else, Daedalus wanted his life to flourish. For many years, their paths had been intertwined. Perhaps now it was time for them to grow apart.

"Certainly his time has come," Daedalus thought to himself. "But there are two paths here and I must not lose sight of my own way." Aside from raising Icarus, building the wings had become the greatest challenge Daedalus had ever undertaken. It was both a cherished recurring dream and the predominating purpose of his waking moments. He had only to close his eyes, anytime, to be able to imagine himself soaring above the island. "The condors do it and some of them are as large as a man. Why should they have the upper air all to themselves?" He dedicated himself to the idea that he would just keep moving towards that end, taking one more step and then another. In the end, it would surely come, the power of soaring on the winds.

And if he built the wings only to fall into the sea, exhausted and too tired to go any further, then at least he would have known the experience of flight. Just imagine how overwhelming it would be to lift up off of the earth for the very first time. That first moment, he would be like a fish jumping into the air and learning for the first time that it had been living within the confines of the water all of its life. It was an odd comparison and he laughed to himself, thinking how much better situated he was than the fish. Not only had he had a good chance to plan for this leap, he could also take comfort in the fact that ever since that first voyage with Icarus across the Aegean Sea to the island, they had both become excellent swimmers. So, Daedalus sat alone on his rock on the

The True Story of Icarus

western edge of the island, musing over the birds and their grace and ease in flight and on his life and the life of his son.

Chapter 24

The Encounter

*There is someone or something which,
once we have come into contact with them or it,
gradually occupies our every thought,
until we can think of nothing else.*
~Paulo Coehlo, The Zahir

The next morning, Icarus made his way to the shallow pool that he heard the night before. Finding it easily, and sensing he was alone, it was time to bath. Grime and sweat had collected on him in thick layers since before he started up the mountain days before. He was not the first to visit the pool that morning. The scent of the goats lingered in the air and their markings littered the smooth rocks around the waters edge. Dropping his gear and his clothes, he waded in, sinking down into the clear sweet coolness of the water.

There was only one way to go from here. He had to follow the gorge out and explore whatever was there, until he came to the sea. Today, he would likely encounter others along the way. Yesterday, he had seen the footprint and there were other signs. The thought of being in contact with people again, after so long in the wilds, pleased him. He was ready to come out. It would be good to meet someone and share some conversation, but the prospect of it made him more than a little nervous. Oftentimes in their travels, he and Daedalus had encountered pleasant people who were willing to share their time, exchange information and even share a meal. It wasn't always that way,

The True Story of Icarus

though. Sometimes, people would go to great lengths to avoid contact. He could remember being camped on a lonely beach with his father and coming upon a man walking through the surf who ran away from them when he first saw them. Two days later, they discovered him following their path at a distance. Strange, that he wanted so much to come closer, but was unable to endure it for very long.

Breaking out of his reverie, Icarus rose up out of the pool and searched for enough sunlight to dry himself and his clothes. Then he gathered up his things, his bow and his knife and the waist kit that held the water bladder, the fishing line and a few other essentials. Refreshed and alert, he made his way down the trail through the gorge, until it gave way and dissolved into an expansive rolling green terrace, sloping downward toward the sea.

He had to stop at the edge of the gorge and take it all in. A small village sat on the edge of a shining blue bay. There were small brown and white houses clustered around a straggle of boats and docks, storage sheds next to humps of rocks covered over with net and bare wooden scaffolding for drying fish. Behind the village a grove of olive trees flourished along the stream bank, ripe and so close at hand. It appeared so peaceful and serene. He wanted to go to the olive trees and pluck some to eat, right away, but he made himself pause. Icarus looked about in all directions, he listened and he smelled. There was a faint sound that made him linger, something he had not heard for many months. It was a beautiful sound and he strained to hear it, pausing still longer just to hear more. Someone was playing a flute.

It was coming from the hillside where sheep grazed. Drawn to the sound, he decided to walk that way, hoping to find a talkative shepherd that would tell him all about this place. As he approached the leeward side of the hill, a dog began to bark and the music abruptly halted. Icarus knew that he had been discovered and looking up he was instantly glad. For there was a young woman holding a flute in one hand and peering at him from the crest of the hill. A small dog stood slightly in front and bared its teeth.

Long dark hair flowed out over her shoulders from beneath the veil she wore over her head. The veil did not cover her face and in the next moment a quiet smile crept into her lips.

Icarus was captivated by the sight of her, unable to move. With that smile, he became instantly aware of an ineffable but universal quality that must have been missing from his life before this.

She looked at him though her dark eyes and half-smiled, as if to say that she too had been waiting for this moment as long as she could remember. He did not look away. It was their moment, complete in itself.

Chapter 25

The Village

*Love is the meaning of life . . .
It is the highpoint of life.*
    ~Joseph Campbell, The Power of Myth

The meeting and lingering of the eyes was just a symptom of the stirring of powerful and surging emotions welling up under the surface. Standing on the flank of the hillside, rooted to the the ground, Icarus felt exposed and uncertain. "At least she has not run away," a nervous Icarus thought to himself and not knowing at all what to do or say, except to return the smile. She did not look away.

He had not seen anyone his age for months, especially not a girl like this one. He waved, still staring, fascinated by the curves of her waist and hips. He was caught up in that uncertain place between intense desire and overwhelming fear; stuck there, unable to move or speak. It was a tension filled place that he knew well, having been a frequent visitor to it when interacting with other girls, back in the time when he and his father lived in the palace. That was in familiar surroundings, with other friends nearby.

Finally the girl turned and broke the gaze. She spoke to the dog and stepped into the shadows on the top of the hill and returned a moment later with her staff in one hand. She smiled again and waved back with the other hand.

A tremendous sense of relief washed over him. That smile, the wave. It was enough, much more than enough to tip the balance of his indecision in favor of desire. His feet and legs propelled him to the top of the hill. For the next several hours, they sat next to one other and told each other their stories.

She told him about each one of the sheep that she tended and the language that they spoke. There was one that always led, another that was the smart one and a another fearful one. She had a story for each of them. Icarus listened to every word, content just to be this close to the beautiful young woman.

For the rest of the day, there was only that young woman with the deep brown eyes, looking deeply into his own, saying the most pointless things, yet fully capable of holding his attention for the rest of his life. When his turn came, he told her about the water in the stream in the gorge coming from melting snows on the tops of the mountains that lay behind them in the clouds and that he had just come from those mountains the day before, drawn by the sound of the gorge to this place by the sea, following her music and now meeting her.

Over the next few days and weeks, Icarus learned that the enchanting young woman was named Sophia and that she and her family lived in a village on a beautiful bay on the southern edge of island. It was far from the palace and the power of King Minos and farther still from the cliff side cave where Daedalus waited.

The village was a cluster of huts made of stone and wood, connected by narrow stone paths and fences and all built around a common circle. There were perhaps one hundred people in all, from the very young to the very old, living off the bounty of the land and sea. They all seemed to be related to one another in some fashion and to him, it is the most beautiful place he had ever been. It is easy for him to reach this conclusion, because he was so completely in love with Sophia. And she with him.

Thoughts of her filled his waking moments and not wanting to leave the village; he began to do whatever he could to contribute. The villagers saw the way that the two looked at one another and did not turn him away. He was young and strong and eager to learn. At first, he went out alone to hunt for his own food. Then, some younger boys from the village asked to go along. After that, two older fishermen of the village offered to take him out in their boat and teach him the ways of fishing in the deep water.

Samir and Ari had known each other all their lives and they always fished together. They took Icarus along with them that day and the next and the one after that. After a short time, Icarus moved his sleeping place to the sand by the boat, instead of alone in the hills beyond the village.

One starry night, while the rest of the village gathered around their central fire for drumming and dancing and storytelling, Icarus and Sophia walked down to the beach together. On this night, he told her about sailing on the wooden ship from Athens as a small boy and growing up on the other side of the island in the palace of the king with his father, Daedalus. He told her about trekking through the wilds in the island's interior, of climbing the mountain that rises at the head of the gorge many miles behind the village and of the cairn of stones that he built at the top. And he told her of looking out from the top of the mountain and of how his eyes kept returning to one gorge that stood out against the backdrop of all the other places to go. It was the one that led to her village. And he told her again of what it felt like to come out of the narrow gorge into the expanse of beautiful lush coastline and to see her there on the top of that hill for the very first time.

Sitting on the sand, she told him her stories of growing up in the village and of the many good memories she had with her family and her friends. She was happy here. It was the only place she had ever lived and the only place she had ever known. She had heard stories told around their community fire, of a large city on the other side of the island, with a palace and a king. But that king, whoever it was, had never come to their village. He had no real power there. The only people she knew with power were the elders of the village. They had been part of the village all of her life. She trusted them and loved them and they returned that love.

One day, while fishing in the deep water, Icarus watched a large, black bird come out of the sky in a slow, ever tightening spiral and descend towards the beach. Samir watched it too and speculated that something large must have washed up on the shore. Ari said it was a good sign and the fishermen were pleased.

They were brown skinned men with strong shoulders and thick arms from pulling on fishing lines and nets, paddling the boat and working with their hands for many days in the sun. Samir was the more demonstrative of the two and the most vocal. He was a younger, shorter version of Ari, both with full heads of dark curly hair and beards. They laughed easily and invited the newcomer to share in their jokes and stories. They had known each other all their lives and could not be closer and they were willing to share their experiences with Icarus.

Samir said that the bird was a condor and that they came down out of the sky, only when there was something very large and tempting for them on the ground, some large fish washed up onto the shore. A whale would be a find indeed, the fat and the bones could be put to many uses and if there was one bird, then there would soon be more. They quickly agreed to bring in the lines and head for shore and to see what the bird was after.

Icarus watched the bird descend on its large black wings and he thought of his father, watching and studying the soaring birds on another side of the island. He knew how pleased Daedalus would be, if he were there. He wanted to get closer, just like Samir and Ari and in that moment, Icarus realized how much he missed his father and it made him sad to think of the separation between them.

How long had he been in the village? The time passed so quickly. The rainy season was ending and it was nearly summer again. Over the weeks and the months since his arrival, he and Sophia had explored many beaches together. They would sit together on the smooth small rocks of the shoreline, long into the night and kiss and he would cradle her head in the crook of one of his strong arms and look into her dark eyes, the smooth brown skin of her face and watch her smile while he gently brushed back her long hair with his fingers.

On the night of the last crescent moon, they walked much farther than before, and found a quiet beach in a hidden cove, far from the village. In the light of that moon, they meandered along the shoreline, touch to touch, their movements a graceful flow. The moon rose higher in the sky, diminishing in size but coming into sharper focus throughout that clear, cloudless night. The crescent shape lay back as if it were a bowl, slightly tipped and full to the brim with a soothing liquid, droplets ready to drip down into the sea.

Bathed in the moonlight, all they could see was each other; it was all they could hear and taste and all they could feel. They moved together on the beach in a graceful, unspoken compromise, matching each others' movement, hand in hand, shoulder to shoulder and thigh to thigh. It was as if there was a shortage of skin; not quite enough for the passion inside, and then not enough air in each breathe.

Until they lay next to each other again, her head on his chest. And she asked him about his father, living in the cave on the western side of the island and of his dream to build wings and to fly away from there. Surely his father had a plan for Icarus to be part of that dream, didn't he?

Icarus replied to her that the only flying that he wanted to do was there in her arms. And they made up their own story about the magic elixir that spilled from the bowl of the crescent moon while they lay in each other arms that night. This particular beach was now their own and they promised each other to return to it and reclaim it, the next time the moon became full of the soothing elixir.

Chapter 26

Sharing the Sky

Forgiveness is sweeping the heart of everything except beauty.
                                                              ~Anonymous

In the next flight dream, the winds aloft were very strong. So strong that they were like a ceiling, keeping Daedalus in the lower elevations and preventing him from pursuing his recurring interest in testing his skills with a flight over the sea. So he turned instead to soaring in the lower levels, discovering what it was like to skim over the land, so close that he could smell the variety in the land as he flew by. Gliding low across the rocky plateaus that night he could see every rock and bush and then he came upon a herd of wild goats descending into a gorge.

Perhaps this was the next lesson presenting itself. He hadn't yet flown into a gorge. What would that be like to feel the walls near at hand while descending into the curving erosional crevice? He took a test run, over flying the length of the gorge just above the trees and tracing the curves of the canyon with his flight path, and found, to his delight, that he could.

Near the bottom of the gorge, where it emptied into the sea, he banked hard to the left and came around through a one hundred and eighty degree turn, returning to his former course and this time moving up the gorge. He dropped down low enough so that he was even with the vegetation on both sides, only slightly above the rim. His vision fixed directly ahead. There was no time to look anywhere else. Then, reaching a wide spot in the canyon, he dropped his elevation, slicing down into the warmer air inside the walls of the gorge. He followed the open air of the canyon in a straight run and just before it curved away in a new direction, he quickly returned to the top of the rim. What a thrill! This brought a whole new intensity to flying.

Keeping his momentum up, he looked ahead and down, watching for and trying to anticipate a good spot for another quick descent. And there is was, right up ahead and the same herd of goats already there and coming into view. They were gradually working their way down towards the flowing water at the bottom. He willed himself to be completely silent as he dropped deeper into the gorge, directing his descending body toward a large male at the back of the herd. At the same moment the goat's ears went to vertical and cocked in different directions, somehow aware that there was a need for vigilance. The goat's head and eyes however, were still lowered, expecting an approach to come from the surface of the earth. It had no experience sensing the approach of a soaring man and Daedalus could not resist the urge to see if could tickle one of the ears as he soared by. And just as the goat loomed large in front of him and his hand reached out to touch the tip of the ear, the goat sensed enough of a presence to bolt to one side, sending all the other goats into a sympathetic sideways rush. Daedalus quickly pulled up and out, escaping from the canyon walls and laughing with delight.

Daedalus watched as the grey and brown rocks passed underneath him, ascending up and out of the steep walled gorge. He became very proficient at piloting himself since the awkwardness of the early dreams. He maneuvered now with confidence and it was so fun to fly. But even though he had become quite skillful at it, there was nothing routine about it. Each time that the flight dream came, it was still a gift and each time that the dream returned, he marveled in it.

Quickly reaching the canyon rim, he continued his ascent, climbing higher into the night sky until he could catch a glimpse of the sea, far in the distance. To his surprise, Daedalus saw that he no longer alone. There in the distance was a winged figure, another person soaring on the winds, so distant that he could barely make it out, but from the shape and they way it moved, it could only be another human. This had never happened before. Always before, he was alone.

Who could it be? Whoever it was, they had seen him too. Daedalus wanted to know and he tried to approach, moving in closer to get a glimpse of who it might be. Each time that he tried to move in closer the other figure receded, keeping the same distance between them.

It went on like that for awhile, matching speed and maneuver and always staying far apart. Then Daedalus decided to change his strategy and instead of trying to approach, he maneuvered into a broad arc which took him steadily away from the flying companion. As he hoped, the other one began to follow, keeping the same distance but now giving chase. He slowed his flight abruptly and the other figure caught up rapidly. Then he abruptly turned and gave chase, driving the other one back and away as fast as the air currents and the gravity fields allowed. It was as if they were children, engaged in a game of tag, or was it cat and mouse.

Whatever the game the novelty eventually gave way to curiosity and they slowly began to approach, their paths parallelled. Each one tracked the other and at the same time deliberately moved in closer and closer. Finally, after much time and maneuvering, the faces came into view.

The face that Daedalus recognized was not someone he would have chosen to share the sky with. It was a woman and not just any woman, but the mother of Talos, the person who more than anyone, was responsible for driving him out of Athens. That was such a painful time in his life that he rarely thought about it. But when he did, the pain was always associated with her.

In recognition, they stared hard at each other, but continued to fly alongside, each one fascinated but wary that the other might venture too close and cause a disastrous collision.

So they flew together that way for a time, matching each

other's speed and direction. There were no taunts or insults and no exchange of words. Neither one of them was interested in revisiting the memories of their old lives back in Athens. The experience of soaring was simply so much better than that. Neither the past nor the future mattered in these moments.

Exchanging glances, they reached a silent understanding that neither one had an interest in the sabotage of the other's flight. There was simply too much at risk. Even the smallest of collisions would cause both of them to lose their forward momentum and neither one wanted to end the flight in a fall to the earth.

Without any sign or signal, the woman shot ahead. Daedalus quickly followed. Still ahead she went into a curve, forcing him to the inside, where he caught up and then overtook her. Then he headed for the shoreline, accelerating as he went just to stay ahead. Reaching the sand, he dropped down so low that he skimmed over the waves. She followed and they soared together in parallel. Then she struck out, setting a tortuous course, daring him to follow. Soon they were carving out parallel trajectories above the island, almost like a dance. Then climbing in a curving spiral, they wove their flight paths together, creating a giant helix in the moonlit sky over the island. Without even speaking other three dimensional designs followed. All they ever communicated was to nod in approval, silently acknowledging the shared beauty of the interwoven contrails.

With that, the mother of Talos turned her head and began a descent somewhere towards the land. With a wave of her hand, she told him not to follow. He returned the wave and watched as she dropped down toward the island. Daedalus soared in a slow circle, watching the descent. He did not follow. Intuitively, he knew that his own flight was also ending and he descended into a broad arc heading for the soft earth of the green field, alone.

Chapter 27

The Choice

*If love is pain,
then it is the pain of being truly alive.*
~Joseph Campbell, The Power of Myth

It was springtime and the days were perfect, endless sun shining down through cloudless deep blue skies. As the days grew longer, the village renewed its custom of gathering in the evenings and watching the sky darken around a common fire. In the gathering darkness, they danced and drummed and told stories under a starry sky.

On the first evening of the first day of Icarus' arrival, Sophia made sure that he was invited to join the evening circle. From the first, he was welcomed into the gatherings, to listen and to talk and to be part of something larger than himself. In this way, he learned about the men and women of the village and they about him. His arrival provided something new and very different. Their's was a small village and of those that were born there, most of them had never traveled more than a few miles from that place. So to many of them, Icarus was from somewhere outside of what they knew and understood, from beyond their edge of outer darkness. In those early days, even with the best of intentions, he could not help being the messenger of both excitement and fear to some. But one thing was clear to the entire village, understood without a single word being spoken. That was his attraction to Sophia and her's for him. Their looks were not lost on anyone, even the children and it served as a perpetual source of interest and speculation.

The True Story of Icarus

The village had its own storyteller; someone with a voice and a willingness to speak, both to entertain and to keep a record of the history of the village. That was the storyteller's gift to the community. Every winter, the elders of the village looked back over the prior year and decided on the one singular event that characterized that year. It was the storyteller's task to develop a story around that event and then to teach the village to remember it by telling the tale, over and over again. In this way each year, the stories became part of the collective memory of the people, part of a larger collection that spanned generations.

The storyteller for the village was Ari, one of the two men that had taken Icarus to learn the ways of fishing from the boat in the deep water. Ari was the quiet one, the observer. On the boat he could be still and composed all day long while Samir sang songs and entertained. But it was Ari that the village gathered around in the evenings, to hear the stories.

After the day in which the condor circled down from the sky right in front of the fishermen, Ari told the story around the village fire. He told them of a large black bird that dropped down to the earth to show the fishermen that something of great interest to a soaring bird had washed up onto the beach. The fishermen turned the boat and brought it in from the deep water, following along the coast of the island until they found the bird again. There it was, a huge black condor, standing astride the broad carcass of a whale, beached on a lonely stretch of shoreline. From the boat they could see the tail of the bloated fish laying stretched out and flat, half in and half out of the water and the bird calmly feeding on the flesh of the exposed back. If the bird had even noticed them, it made no sign.

They took the boat down wind until they found a protected place to set the anchor and then the two older men silently slipped over the side and waded through the water leaving Icarus to catch up. Not a word had been spoken between them and not wanting to be left behind, Icarus quickly followed.

Once on the beach, Icarus quickly caught up with them and then kept going, running faster and faster across the rocky pebbles, right until he turned a corner of a large rock face and the overpowering smell of their quarry stopped him in his tracks; but he did not turn away. He was stunned by the sheer size of the dead whale, that and the smell and the presence of the large bird perched on his back. Samir caught up and asked him if he thought the bird had ridden on the whale's back, right up onto the beach.

"It could have happened," Samir said, grabbing the younger man by the shoulder. The three of them watched for a while, not wanting to disturb the feasting bird. The head was turned just a little bit away, the way bird's do when they want to keep something in full view. And it was watching them closely.

The bird's talons held fast to the whale's flesh and it had a strong curving beak for tearing into flesh, fully capable of closing and ripping out large chunks. The men waited and watched, fascinated to be so close to the feasting bird that watched them with a corresponding intensity.

After a time, Samir saw no reason to be restrained any longer and he stepped forward into the smell of the beached whale and toward the huge bird. At the first movement, the bird turned its bald head just enough to glare at the approaching man. His arms gesturing wildly and breaking into a song that rose over the sound of the waves, Samir lunged forward. At what seemed the last possible second, a broad expanse of wings unfolded from the bird's body. At the same time, it braced itself, digging its claws deeper into the flesh and then sprang upwards from that fixed position, launching itself straight upwards several meters off of its meal. Samir leapt too but quickly fell back to the earth, calling out to the huge bird to take him along and show him what it would be like to fly away on the winds. At the top of its leap, the bird extended its wings and flapped them just enough to face into the steady breeze. Then looking down at Samir it loosed a discharge from its rear, demonstrating its position on the matter. The wings flapped gently again against the underlying column of air and the bird rose, caught by the breeze and instantly pushed away

The True Story of Icarus

from the beach, the men and the meal, gliding off, faster and higher than any pursuer could possibly go. Once again in the sky, the bird was king.

The three men stood on the beach in silence. They could not help but watch the bird glide away, lost in the wonder of what they had seen. To see such a huge bird leap into the sky like that, so close at hand and then to see it fly through the air right before their eyes and with such grace and agility. The wings were as long as the sail of their boat. It was a beautiful sight to behold.

That night, back at the village, the strips of whale blubber that they had cut away from the carcass were boiled down into a light oil that would have many uses. But Icarus was not there to hear the words or to be part of the drumming that would follow. He did not want to stay and be part of the gathering that night. The events of the day had taken him inward. There was just not enough splendor in the stars or the sea that night, to take his attention away.

He thought about all the promises he had made, the commitments. It seemed as if he was carrying a great weight and that no matter what happened now, he could not be everything that all the important people in his life were expecting. So many promises made, spoken and unspoken. There were the passion driven ones he had made to Sophia and the unspoken ones made to Samir, Ari and the rest of the villagers that he wanted to be one of them. And of course the one he had apparently forgotten, made to Daedalus all those months before; that he was on a quest to find a glue for the wings and that he would one day return. And what of his role in his father's dream for leaving the island in the hope of finding a better place. The thought of it made him wince. "Oh father," he thought. "Would you understand if you knew how good it is to be here?"

He could hear a little boy inside somewhere, telling him that he could just run away from it all and be done with it. He could still put it all behind him and find pleasure somewhere else, run away and back to the high plateaus, all alone and into the wild, the way it had been a few months before. There he could be free again, no more promises but his own.

To have that kind of freedom meant living alone. Being with Samir and Ari and the other villagers, showed him that he wanted so much more than a life of isolation could provide. He knew then what he wanted and it was not the life that his father envisioned for him. Being with Sophia had taught him that. He wanted to marry her and live by the sea in a tiny village and fish and hunt and join in that community. Even if that meant that he would never again venture more than a few miles from that place. He believed that he could be very happy living that life. And with that clarity, Icarus was at peace with himself once again.

His thoughts went back to the condor on the beach and its flight into the sky. What if it was a messenger, reminding him that it was time to go back to his father and explain. The rainy months were ending and it was the perfect time to travel. He understood now that it was time for him to go back. A whole year was nearly passed since they had left the palace together. He would have to tell Daedalus that they would not be leaving the island together and he had no idea at all how to do that. It was something he knew very clearly that he had to do, but just as strongly, he knew that he did not want to disappoint his father.

He walked along the shore that night for a long time, thinking of the dilemma and the words he might say. It simply came down to a choice, his choice to go in a different direction, one that gave him meaning and purpose. He wanted to marry Sophia and make a life with her and her people. All night, he walked along the shore alone thinking and hoping that surely his father would understand, until the sun and the birds awoke and the day appeared.

Chapter 28

The Gift

*Manhood emerges when the person you wish to be,
comes into precise accord,
with the person you must be.*
~Peter Charles Melman, The Landsman

    Several weeks later, Icarus and Sophia were in the fishing boat, tacking to the West, into the wind and looking for the barren cliff where Daedalus waited and made his home. With them they carried a several urns, centered in the boat for balance. Glancing from the tiller at the graceful curve of the largest urn, Icarus wondered if the contents would be enough to carry all the hopes and dreams that were poured into it. In the bow, Sophia faced the water and played on her flute. She made music and another graceful curve to occupy his attention.
    In the low afternoon light, he thought that he recognized the rocky promontory that marked the location of the cave, where many months before he made his home with his father. He was almost sure this block of vertical rock was the right one. So many memories of their time together all came flooding back. Icarus was excited to be returning and he scanned the rocky slopes, trying to catch a glimpse of the old man, his father. He was glad to be making the trip with his new wife.
    Sophia could sense his excitement and she had some of her own. She had never been this far from her village before, so it was an adventure for her. But they had been on the water a full

Daedalus Rising

day and she was more than ready to find the place, get out of the boat and start the reunion.

They had married the week before. It took the village three full days, from start to finish to get through all the ritual and celebration in order to create a couple. By the time it was through, there was no doubt in anyone one's mind that these two individuals were now united and a couple with its own identity.

Icarus was pleased with the marriage and proud of his new wife. He was glad to have her along. Of course, he wanted her to meet his father, but he also wanted Daedalus to understand both his reasons and the depths of his desire to stay on the island.

The familiar looking rock face came closer and Icarus felt his excitement rise. Even before they were within calling distance, he was on his feet, wanting to call out. The boat seemed to crawl across the water. Finally, as they drew nearer, Icarus knew that it was the right rock and he said to Sophia, "This is it. I know this is the one." Then he called out, "Daedalus! Father! Are you there? Hello!"

There was no response and no movement on the shore. The small boat moved past the rock face and continued up the shore, toward a tidal pool with quiet water that Icarus had fished from many times. Sophia looking astern and saw a figure come out onto the top of the cliff and wave. She waved back and asked, "Is that him? Turn around, quick."

Icarus jumped up, keeping one hand on the tiller. He waved and shouted at his father. Daedalus waved back, returning an unintelligible and extremely exuberant shout. Then he disappeared behind the rock face, making for the trail that led to the shore and the base of the cliff. From that point on, the minutes seemed to crawl as they made for the safe mooring. Daedalus was already on the beach, jogging to catch up.

"You're pretty fast for an old man," Icarus called out from the boat.

"It's good to see you too," he shouted back.

The True Story of Icarus

Daedalus ran ahead to the tidal pool and watched the boat come in. This was not the homecoming he had expected. He always thought that when Icarus returned, it would be over land, a goat or a deer over his shoulders to feast upon. At last, he stood up to his knees in the quiet water, tears streaming down his face watching his son bring a sailboat in through the surf with beautiful dark haired young woman in the bow. Daedalus had no idea that he even knew how to sail. Obviously, there were many things he did not yet know about his son. What he did know and all that really mattered in that moment was that his son had returned and by all appearances, a happy man. This was more than enough and Daedalus was happy too. His heart was so filled with joy that he placed his hand over it and held it there, as if it were bursting. With tears streaming down his face, he stood there and waited his arms open and outstretched. With some difficulty, he managed to say, "Welcome back. Welcome back."

Icarus jumped off the boat and high stepped through the water. He wrapped his arms around the man's waist, picked him up and carried him up to the beach, swinging his father around something like a rag doll. Sophia watched and smiled, happy herself to be able to be in that moment. Once Icarus set his father down, she walked over to join them. A little uncertain, she put her hand on Icarus' shoulder. He turned quickly and smiled. Introductions were made and Daedalus, surprised with this unexpected development, quickly adjusted and included her in the welcoming. From what he had observed from the way of things, he already understood a great deal and it created a pang of regret for him, even in this joyous moment. He already sensed that there would not be a need for two sets of wings. And it turned out to be a pain easily released, because so much more than that, was the love that he had for his son. He was healthy and happy and he had returned. That was really all there needed to be in this moment. The rest would come later.

"Welcome, welcome, welcome," Daedalus said, again clapping his hands on his son's shoulders and holding him in his gaze. "You came back. It feels like a long time that I have waited for this moment." And then glancing at Sophia to include her in the thought, "And you return with a beautiful girl by your side. What could be better?"

"Sophia is my wife, father," Icarus replied. "And you are right, I am happy. And there is so much to tell, I don't know where to start."

"Then come, both of you. Come up to the camp, both of you. You must be hungry. We will make a fire and talk and eat and toast to our good fortune. To help pass the time, I've been experimenting with wine making."

"You go first father. I need to go back and get some things from the boat."

"Let me help then," offered Daedalus.

"No. Not yet. You will ask too many questions." Icarus responded. "Sophia and I will follow you up to the cave."

So Daedalus went first and soon began stoking up the fire. There was so much he wanted to say and he had no idea where to start, but there would be plenty of time for that. It was better to let Icarus be the center of attention, for him to tell his stories. Daedalus was eager to hear them all. He looked up to see his son and his wife walking towards him down the trail, carrying between them a large, colorful urn. "They move together very well," he nodded to himself.

A short time later, Icarus became the first storyteller, beginning with the story of climbing the snow capped mountain and from there discovering the way to the gorge that led to the village where Sophia and her people lived. He skipped right past the part about meeting Sophia and began telling of the village and the people, how they lived and what an ideal place it was.

"So tell me your story," Daedalus interrupted. "That's what I want to know first. How did you two meet?"

And smiling at both of them, Sophia told them of seeing a wild man that came out of the gorge one day, while she was tending her sheep. This wild man started to chase after the poor frightened animals, but she quickly grabbed her staff and ran to the animals aid, chasing him back up into the gorge, shaking her staff at the wild man and promising that he would get much worse if he ever tried to come back. Then she returned to her flock, only to be surprised a short time later by a gentle and handsome young man who came striding down from the gorge, calling himself Icarus. And he walked right up to her, smiled and stole her heart. Finishing the tale, Sophia clapped her hands and laughed at her story as the fire danced and crackled. They all joined in.

"I'm so glad that you came all the way out here from your village, Sophia. It pleases me to see my son so happy."

Icarus reached for her hand and took hold of it. He looked over at his father and told him that they celebrated their marriage in the village at the last full moon. Then he blurted out, "Father! Even if you can show me how to fly, I am staying here. That is your dream. I have found my own and it is with Sophia in her village."

"Somehow, I knew that already," said Daedalus, looking back into his son's gaze, "and I understand, more than I can explain."

"But think about this," Icarus responded, "You can return there with us. The villagers will welcome you. The elders have made that very clear."

Sophia nodded.

"It is a beautiful place and I know you could be happy there." Icarus went on. "You don't have to leave the island anymore. Do you? You could return to the village and make it your home."

Daedalus smiled and said nothing for awhile. He tried to imagine himself as a fisherman in a small village by the water. He closed his eyes and tried to form the image in his head, but it didn't seem to fit. Instead he thought about the flight dream and the grace and elegance of soaring on the winds. He could see the shadow of his winged body moving across the ground, as he soared above the edge of the cliff looking down at the sea.

He had been alone on the cliff by the sea for many months and in that time, he had often thought of Icarus' return. He missed him and he missed the company. And lately, in his own dreams, he had seen his son with long white wings on his shoulders and arms, soaring over the ocean. It was a dream of flight and a dream of change and in it Daedalus would mount his own set of wings and rush to join Icarus in the air. As always, it was wonderful to soar through the air and feel the power of flight, but in the dream Icarus was always far ahead and although Daedalus tried mightily, he could not catch up. And when he awoke after first having that dream he concluded optimistically that he only just needed a little more time and that eventually they would fly together.

Now he understood that the dream carried a different message. It was not the outcome Daedalus expected; but then again, he was the one that sent Icarus off on a quest, and given him his blessing. Who could know how he would return? So Daedalus knew that he could not impose his own expectations on the outcome that had appeared at the door that day. Icarus had been tested in ways that Daedalus would never know and now he was returned with a design for his own life. If this was what his son wanted, then as far as Daedalus was concerned, he made some fine choices.

This was not the boy that left his home all those months before. Daedalus could still remember the words that he spoke to Icarus then; "That no matter what happened, you must return and when you do come back, no matter how or what, you will be welcome." Daedalus had no idea at the time, the depth of his own profundity. But it was certainly coming home to him now. He stood up and walked around the fire so that he stood behind and between Icarus and Sophia. He placed his arms around both of their shoulders, giving each the strongest hug he could manage. He made Sophia blush telling her how much he had always wanted a daughter. And now he had one. Then he embarrassed Icarus by telling him how proud he was and glad too, that both of them had come home.

The True Story of Icarus

Daedalus returned to his seat and talked for awhile about the wings, his fascination with the condors and how it takes a huge wingspan to hold such a large bird in the air. Icarus responded by telling the story of finding one of the condors feeding on the carcass of a whale on the beach while fishing with his friends Samir and Ari. Daedalus wondered if it could have been the one he called Basia, or maybe one of the parents. He had spent so much time studying and admiring them from afar. Icarus had managed to get face to face with one of them.

They talked and laughed late into the night and when the moon was high overhead Daedalus started to yawn. At that, Icarus feigned impatience, pointedly asking, "Aren't you going to ask about the quest. You do remember the quest, don't you?"

"I thought you reinvented it and brought back a girl, a woman, instead." Daedalus replied, completely serious.

"No father, that's not it at all. The glue that you sent me to find is in the urn that we carried just now from the boat. I would have never found it without Sophia and the rest the villagers." Icarus replied with sincerity. "I didn't want to return until the quest was complete."

Icarus picked up the heavy clay urn and set it in front of his father. Daedalus ran his fingertips over the hard dark shell that had formed on the top, then he rapped on it with his knuckles. He didn't understand what it was that he was looking at yet, but tears were running down his cheeks again anyway. He looked at the urn and then hugged his son and after thanking them both and asked, "Okay, so what is this stuff?"

This was the moment that Icarus had waited for and he wanted to savor it. He began again, talking about fishing on the boats and the size of the fish that they sometimes go after. To catch the big fish, they often go far out beyond the sight of land and sometimes they encountered storms. In order to keep the boats seaworthy, the villagers make a sealant when they have the right materials. And this past spring, we were able to make some. He told Daedalus how the villagers all gathered together one evening, just a few weeks before and boiled down bits of the whale's flesh to make a fine oil for burning in their lamps. Then they set some of the oil aside and mixed it with beach tar and bits of ground up sea urchin spine and other ingredients that he could also only guess at and heated them in a huge copper pot over the fire. He told of how the mixture became a liquid and how the villagers took turns stirring and stirring, until it was finally ready. Then the boats were hauled up onto the sand and the keels painted with the hot liquid. And the whole time the entire village chanted and drummed for the safe return of the boats and everyone in them. It was a beautiful thing watch."

Icarus paused, smiled at Sophia and then continued, "When I saw the hot liquid transform into a hardened blank shell, I knew that it had to be the perfect glue for your wings."

Daedalus' became serious now. Turning to his son and seeing the look of satisfaction on his face, he knew that Icarus truly believed the words he was saying. Daedalus said nothing, but nodded, encouraging his son to continue.

"Many times around the fire, I told the villagers my stories of growing up with you and how we once lived as caged Athenian birds in the palace of Minos, but finally left in order to discover our freedom. They approved of what you did, of what we did."

"That's reassuring," thought Daedalus to himself.

"And of course I told them what happened to us since then. How we came to live on another side of the island, near a cave that you stuffed completely full of feathers, studying birds and with a dream of designing and building wings to fly off of this island. Father, when I saw the sealant and what it did to the boats, I knew it had to be just what you were searching for and I told them so."

"They must think that I am crazy," said Daedalus.

"Some of them do. But they have never seen a flying man before; so it is difficult for them to believe," replied Icarus, slapping him on the shoulder. "But whether they believed you to be crazy or not, all of them were willing to help."

The True Story of Icarus

"We made a big batch for you and your wings," said Sophia. "But not in the usual way. Yours was different. After the tars and the oils were heated together in the big pot over the fire, we added different ingredients, special ones, for you and your flight over the water; dried powder from an eagle's heart, small pieces of condor tail feather and other things only the elders can know."

"It was a beautiful sight to see the entire village dancing and singing around the fire that night, chanting for you father. To give you courage and direction, skill and fortitude and fair winds. It will be a lonely journey and like no other," said Icarus, mixing pride and sadness with the words.

Daedalus stared into the fire, speechless. The incredible magnitude of this gift was slowly dawning on him. It was like the realization of a dream. He saw it all like a huge tapestry. Icarus had gone not just to find the glue, but for meaning in his own life. And he found those things and more. Here he was, not just with the glue, but with the blessings and prayers of an entire village of people. People he did not even know wanted him to succeed in his own quest. What an incredible gift it was. This was the key to realizing the dreams of flight that had been coming to him for all these years. And all he had to do was reach out and take it. His son, in completing his own quest, was showing Daedalus the way to continue on his own path, if that was indeed what he still wanted for his life.

"I'm overwhelmed with what you have done."

Icarus came over and stood behind his father, his hands on his shoulders. "Father," he said, "you have been blessed by the village."

"I have been blessed by all of you."

It was such a joy filled moment. They all cried and then they toasted one another, mixing the tears with the wine. "I have never felt so full, so happy, as I do right now," said Daedalus. He thanked them both for all they had done. And he told them to thank the villagers too. That their gift was a huge step along the path of his own journey and that they were very thoughtful, generous and kind.

Daedalus Rising

Icarus asked his father if he wanted to return with them to the village and tell them himself. "You don't have to fly off to another island." He told his father with all the sincerity he could muster. "You could live out your days in the village in peace."

Daedalus thought about it long into the night. It was an appealing thought. He would be able to watch Icarus grow and be the man he was becoming. And he imagined that it would not take long before they had children of their own and Daedalus knew he would enjoy being a grandfather. But he also wondered how happy he could really be, living in a quiet fishing village, surrounded by so many people he had never known before.

As appealing as it seemed at first blush, he knew that it was not his path, just as surely as Icarus must have known when he went to the village in the first place. Daedalus had a calling, a personal legend. It was to soar on the winds, on wings of his own design and this was his opportunity to do it. There would never be another time like this time and all that he had to do was accept the glue and then build them. Just as it was promised in the dream so long ago.

There were many reasons to support his decision. For another, Minos would not have forgotten. By now there was surely a reward for both of them. If he, Daedalus, went to the village, how long would it take before a traveler or a sailor from outside would visit and stay long enough to learn about one or both of them. The king had many eyes and ears and eventually, word of their location would travel back to Minos, particularly if the way was paved with gold. Daedalus could just picture Minos planning his revenge. He would send soldiers or ships or both and that would be the end of them. The entire village might be in jeopardy.

And Daedalus could not let that happen. Icarus and Sophia deserved to have a safe and stable place to raise their family. That would be his gift to them in return.

Long after Icarus and Sophia had fallen asleep, Daedalus made his plans; not just for the construction of the wings, but also to keep the village safe from the vengeance of the king. When he finally dozed, he dreamt of small happy children playing in a gentle surf near a quiet fishing village by the sea.

Chapter 29

Taking Off

I know that I have the best of time and space-
And that I was never measured and never will be measured.
~Walt Whitman, Leaves of Grass

After sipping tea brewed over an early morning fire, Daedalus showed them the prototype. It lay on a patch of level ground at the base of a high grassy hill, not far from the cave. He had been waiting a long time to show his creation to someone. For many months, he had only himself to talk with, about the vital connection between the wings and the body. Now Icarus was here and Sophia too, both brimming with their youthful fires and natural curiosity. He stepped into the inventor role one more time, relishing it like never before and explaining the process of assembling all the pieces and how it would all work.

In the months while Icarus was away, Daedalus filled many of his days with a single minded intensity, gathering together all that he would need for flight from the island, to become a flying man. He never doubted that in some fashion, it would all come together. To gain the extra length needed for a proper wing span, he constructed a lightweight external framework of native woods, bone and leather, just large enough to enclose his own chest and link the weight of his hips to the wings.

The wings of course needed feathers, many different ones, positioned and woven together for maximum strength and support. This would be his greatest invention, his masterpiece.

The True Story of Icarus

And over the months, he collected enough parts to build, not just one, but two sets of wings. His plan was to build one pair, test it and then incorporate improvements into the second set. Of course, there was no need now for the second pair of wings but still there were lots of spare parts. He gave them to Icarus with a smile and a wink, suggesting that he might change his mind later and want to build another set of wings some day.

So they stoked up the fire, cracked open the urn and began the liquefaction process. Eventually the stiff, tarry mixture gave way to a glossy black liquid that bubbled in the heat. All that day they labored together and the next and next. For Daedalus, it was the culmination of a lifetime of experiences coming together, focused onto a singular point in time and what a joy, an absolute joy to share it with Icarus. It was a numinous time and in whatever time that it took, the three of them created a huge pair of formidable wings.

After a short celebration, they agreed that the wings had to be tested right away. So they carried them to the top of the treeless hill and set them on the ground. Sophia and Icarus each held onto one side while Daedalus wriggled into the frame. Then he lay there face down upon the ground, extending the arms and the reach of his fingers out into the grips on each wing. Straddling him, Icarus laced the two sides of the back together with leather straps, joining the symmetrical halves together at the seam that ran along Daedalus' back.

Daedalus had taken off and flown so many times in his dreams. Surely there was no reason to be nervous about it now, but he was. His mind raced with a hundred reasons to stay, a thousand things he had not yet considered and they were all flooding into his head at once. His stomach churned. Then the memory of a dream came back to him, one from many years before. Not a flight dream, but a dream about a gift and a commitment that he made. The pledge he had made to be willing to receive a great gift and not be too busy or too tired or too afraid.

Icarus' voice was behind him, "Are you ready to stand up?"

He nodded his head and struggled to raise himself on one foot and then the other.

With Icarus and Sophia steadying him, Daedalus stood on the hillside the wind in his face. He studied the feel of the wings, contracting his hands and extending his arms. Then he gently rotated his arms and shoulders, testing the resistance of the wind as he moved them into and out of the flow.

"We have come very far, you and I," he said to Icarus, his face beaming.

"Yes, I know. How do the wings feel?"

"Let me go and we'll find out."

As he said those words, the two sets of hands that tethered the wings let go and Icarus and Sophia stepped back, disappearing from view. He felt himself immediately buffeted about as the wings caught the winds, a nervous kind of energy that conveyed a sense of urgency for movement and flight. He had to step quickly from side to side just to keep his balance and not fall. With his feet already in motion, he started, bouncing rapidly down the hill in quick short steps. As his feet moved him down the hill, his palms opened upwards and the shoulders rotated back, finding the place where the lift was maximized. He held it there as best he could, feeling the support of the column of air that was pushing and lifting. Dropping his weight down onto his left leg, he pushed off, extending his right and giving himself a strong push up and off the ground, trusting that the winds would catch the wings and hold him. . . and they did.

The winds caught and lifted him upwards into the air, higher and back towards the top of the hill. It all happened so fast that by the time he leveled off and could look down again, he could see Icarus and Sophia far below waving and cheering. Then they were hugging each other and jumping up and down. They shouted and pointed up at him. He wanted very badly to wave back but all he could do was nod and to shout out his own joy filled laugh. It was even better than in the dream.

Rolling the shoulders slightly forward, he tested the currents and his ability to glide, the way he had done in the dream time

The True Story of Icarus

so many times before. He searched for an updraft. Many times he watched the soaring birds catch thermals in the early morning air as the sun heated up the land. Gliding past the cliff face that marked his home he found it, rising up off the ocean's edge. Gently the air seemed to push from below as he banked and rolled into a slow upward spiral, just as he had done so many times before in the dreams. He watched the ground recede and the two uplifted faces on the hillside growing smaller and smaller. The sun was warm on his head and shoulders drawing him upward, higher and higher. It was so like the dream, only better.

He rose with the thermal until he had gained enough elevation to make his way back to the hillside to where his family waited. Then he rolled out of the uplift and let the currents of the prevailing wind push him back to them, soaring along in slow motion just like the condors that he admired so much. He wished that one was in the air today to see this.

"Too bad," he thought, "any bird sharing the air with a flying man would certainly have a story to tell."

As he neared the grassy hill, he brought the wings in, as much as their design would allow and brought his body back to the earth in as steady a descent as he could maintain. His plan was to stall the glide somewhere near the top of the hill and then drop to the earth. Landing, he soon discovered was part of the challenge. He came in faster than he expected and a little ways down on the hillside. Touching down he was instantly scrambling to keep on his feet. The ground was not level and try as he might, he could not keep his balance. He fell forward hard, spread eagled and planting his face and chest squarely into the earth of the hillside. It was a graceless landing but he was far more concerned about damage to the wings than himself. Icarus and Sophia were soon there, helping him up, brushing the dirt from his face and chest.

"Are you alright?" Icarus asked.

"I have never felt better."

"It was beautiful," said Sophia. "All of it."

Daedalus Rising

That night they grilled sea bass over the fire, shared more wine and watched the sun go down from the top of the cliff. Daedalus watched it many times from that vantage point, Icarus too; but it was still something unique. Daedalus was leaving soon. So this night, they feasted and toasted and they put their arms around each others shoulders and danced together on the top of the rock with the rising moon and as if there would be no tomorrow. Because this was Daedalus' last night on the island, their last time together and of that, they were all keenly aware.

It was an extraordinary event and Daedalus wanted to make it a wonderful memory. He needed that, because right up until that afternoon, the day when the wings would actually be finished only got closer and closer, but never arrived. Now it was here and Daedalus had to say good-bye for the last time, to the one person that he cared about more than anyone else. He learned just how difficult the receipt of a truly magnificent gift can be.

The next morning when the sun rose, they drank tea together and ate a small breakfast. If he was going to do this thing, then he did not want to wait. The wind was perfect and he felt strong. The sun was warming the earth and thermals of heated air would soon be rising. He would find another and rise with it higher and higher, like the big predator birds, until he was high enough to see all around in every direction. Then he would select his course to the next island, gliding on the winds until he made his way to that far shore.

They sat together on the hillside and had one last conversation. Daedalus reminded his son of the promise he had made back in the harbor in Athens, to protect him, keep him safe and see that he was never hungry.

"Yes, and you did all those things. I will never forget you."

"It was the best thing that I ever did," replied his father.

"What about inventing the wings?" Icarus wanted to know.

"They are wonderful aren't they? You must try it someday,

both of you. Now listen to me, please. These wings are wonderful creations, but Icarus, you must understand how it all came about. To build these wings I had to reach very deep and very far beyond the things that I ever expected for myself. I would not have found the dedication needed for reaching them, without you."

Icarus blushed and Daedalus continued, "If not for you, I would still be back in the city right now, building a temple for king Minos and asking myself why designing buildings never seemed like enough. You were the motivation to keep going towards this deeper purpose, this wonderful creation. Because of you, I have kept on my path and all because of that promise I made to you long ago."

"I remember."

With their help, Daedalus began wriggling into the wings one more time. Soon they finished and he smiled at each of them saying, "Well, thank you both for the wonderful gift. May you always care for one another and make lots of good memories. And tell your children all about this day and the man their grandfather was."

Icarus told him that when Minos was gone and it was safe, that he must come back to the island, find their village and that they would be waiting for him this time. Sophia promised him that when he did return to the island, the village would throw a weeklong celebration for the return of the flying man. They exchanged clumsy hugs at the top of the hill, one last time.

Then from the high grassy knoll, Daedalus took the first steps of the next leg of his journey. These particular steps were met by a rushing wind and his wings spread and caught the updraft. Daedalus let the current wash over him. It carried him higher and higher above the island. He saw Icarus and Sophia watch and wave and cheer as he rose, until they became round specks in the middle of a green patch of earth. He ascended, looking for that high place in the sky to find the bearing he needed to locate the next island. He would follow that bearing, the sun on his shoulders and the past slipping away.

Chapter 30

The Flight

*Forget about faith.
You don't need faith to fly,
You need to understand flying.*
~Richard Bach, Messiah's Handbook

    He rode the thermal high above the island, many hundreds of feet up and there he found a river of wind, deep and wide blowing to the north. He found a balance within the currents and became part of the flow. There was no sound when he traveled with it, but the winds roared and pulled at him when he banked the wings against them. The winds carried him along the western edge of the island. The sun rose up over his right shoulder and cast a huge moving shadow on the water below. It was his shadow, a flying man. He watched with intense interest as the silhouette moved across the water. It was a sublime experience, balanced on the wings of his own creation, between the soaring heights and the great depths. Nothing in the flight dreams prepared him for this.

    In the early morning sunlight, he watched the coast line slip away and fall behind. The winds carried him out beyond the land and he was high above the open water, still moving north, the sky and sparkling sea blending into an ever deepening blue.

    Far ahead and to the west, a brownish green mass came into his field of view. If he stayed in the river of wind, he would pass it by, far to the east of the island. To break away from the current would take a great deal of effort and then he would still

The True Story of Icarus

have to cover a lot of open ocean just to reach it. So he rode along on the winds for a time, considering the options and as he thought about it, another island appeared. This one far to the east; and that was the answer. There would be more islands and as long as his shoulders maintained and the winds held, then he would stay aloft and surely reach another. It was a beautiful day for soaring and no reason for haste. Then the first island passed from view but another one took its place, just below the horizon and beckoning him on.

Several hours later, he passed over another island, this one directly below. His shoulders were growing heavy and it did not appear to be inhabited. There were no houses and no boats. If there were no people, then there was probably no water. That would not be a safe place to land. Besides that, in order to carry out his plan, there had to be people around to watch and see that a man had flown. He would keep going until he found the one that was right for his purpose, and stay aloft a while longer, most of the day if he had too.

His body was growing stiff and weary. The sun was high overhead. Its light surrounded him, warmed him and helped to keep his spirits up. All alone in an endless sky, he was beginning to tire. The intense stimulation and excitement of soaring was gone. That was not the way it was in the last flight dream, the one in which the mother of Talos put him through his paces.

"There was an irony," he thought to himself. "The most challenging and demanding flying I ever dreamt and Talos' mother was right there with me, my partner. Where is she today?" he asked with a sardonic laugh. "I could use the company."

He could not let go of the memory of that particular dream and the more he thought about it, the more her being there, made sense. She was the one who started him on his path. Without her in his life he would never have left Athens, never have known Icarus, never have learned about the richness of a father's love for a child and never have experienced the beauty of flying. In her way, she was part of this gift. He might even be thankful that she came into his life. The experiences that he most valued, all seemed to developed out of the encounter with her.

There was nothing ironic about her presence in the dream at all. She had to be there and for the first time in his life, he felt grateful for what she had done to him, and for him. With that realization, he saw that he was no longer so alone. After all, he had the hopes and prayers of an entire village in the air, soaring right along with him. The mother of Talos was his teacher and her lesson was of the power of forgiveness.

By the time the next island came into view, he was tired, very tired. His arms and shoulders were leaden and all that he could feel was his desire to stop and rest. His eyes burned and blinking did not take away the dry ache. The sun was long past its zenith. "This island has to be the one," he thought.

As the distance closed, he watched as the island took shape and enlarged, taking up more space upon the water. The details of the topography slowly came into view. He could see the green forests and hills, a river channel that originated in high peaks clustered in the island's center and square patches of fields clustered around a large village on its south end. Two fishing boats were making their way into the harbor at day's end. "This was it," he said, feeling a wave of relief coming over him. With the sun on his left shoulder, Daedalus set his mark on the center of the village and began his gradual descent.

Still several kilometers out, he slipped down through the layers of air in a broad arc, his trajectory like an arrow descending to its intended target. And like the arrow, his speed increased. At first, he was too tired to respond to the downward acceleration, but he could not ignore it for long. He knew what had to happen. He had to rotate his exhausted shoulders back and down in order for the wings to brace against the air beneath them and slow his descent. But he could not, his arms and shoulders would not respond. The air grew steadily warmer as the land rose up towards him as if in some kind of greeting. It was the inexorable attraction of the earth, not willing to be denied any longer.

He realized now that when he first took off back on the island, he had not completely worked out the details of the landing. He imagined himself dropping in for a graceful but dramatic finish, landing upon a promising island in the middle of an excited village full of appreciative people and celebration. According to the original, optimistic plan, his arrival was something the villagers could not help but notice. Something so unusual, that they would tell of it for years to come, the story of the flying man and of his flight to their island. Crashing exhausted into the middle of the village was not the outcome he wanted. Nor was ditching the flight far out at sea. If he decided on that course, there was a good chance no one would ever notice him. And for his plan to work, there had to be people to see it all happen.

He tried to level the wings and hold some elevation, slowing the downward descent enough to regain some control. But each time that he tried to hold on, the weariness gripped his back and shoulders. The muscles were heavy and barely responsive. He was coming in like a falling star from the heavens. "There was some beauty in that," he thought. "But it is not the ending I want for my story."

He was so close, there had to be a way to finish it. That was what mattered, to complete the journey he began so long ago. With the earth rising higher, he realized that the quality of the landing did not matter at all, so long as he made one. All the rest was his own vanity. He just needed to finish and survive and that would be enough. The one thing that mattered was to get someone in the village to notice, to get their attention. A man with wings soaring over their village would surely be enough.

As the distance closed, he could make out individual homes and see villagers moving about. To land in their midst he would have to slow himself to a stall, then pull up for a graceful drop to the earth. It was out of the question. He was coming in far too fast. The best he could hope for was to avoid hitting the houses. So he brought himself down above the main street, coming in fast. Over the center of town, he managed to roll his exhausted torso into a banked turn, gliding past the roofs high enough to clear and then extending the wings through the arc of the turn and holding it long enough to set the wings on a course for the harbor.

They saw him. Even his ears seemed tired but as he passed overhead, he could hear them shouting at him, some of them cheering. Several people stood below and looked up at him and pointed to the sky. He could feel their sense of wonder as it reached up and out to him, even as his own heart went out to them, thanking them for just being there.

More people followed, coming out of their homes, pointing to the sky and calling out to still more. Some of them were following, running towards the harbor and trying to catch up. No one wanted to miss a single moment.

Coming out of the turn, he found a slight breeze blowing gently into him off the water. He balanced the wings into it, using it as best he could to slow himself still more. Past the town now and headed for the sea, Daedalus closed his eyes, giving in to the fatigue. He opened them again, in time to see a fishing boat coming into the harbor, the setting sun directly behind. What a pretty image it was. And he thought of his father and when he was a young boy. He pictured his father's face and imagined his presence somewhere nearby. There seemed to be another shadow presence behind him, his grandfather, a man he had never met. And there were other deeper shadows, more grandfathers and ancestors, all gathered around him and following his path. They watched him and held him up, just as they had all through the flight that day, guiding him to the island, through the final turn over the village and now out over the harbor.

Not far above the water now, the flying man shot past the fishing boats. His eyes were shut tight, but he thought that he could still hear cheering people jumping upon the wooden

The True Story of Icarus

decks, slapping the sides of the boats with their hands and calling out to him. The water was very close now. He could feel it pulling him in. But he was much too tired to look, too tired to do anything except trust in the choice of landing sites and trust that someone from the village would be there in time; because he had to lay down now and rest for awhile.

Chapter 31

The Return

A man's work is nothing but a slow trek to rediscover through the detours of his art, those one or two images in whose presence, his heart once opened.

~Albert Camus

Gravity finally prevailed, pulling his body out of the sky and into the sea. The tip of the left wing hit first and took a lot of the impact, breaking apart and shattering into many pieces. Then the rest of him cartwheeled into the water. Several fisherman stood up in their boats, staring in disbelief. Right in front of their eyes and not so many feet away, a winged man had just soared passed the town and tried to make a water landing. The best swimmer amongst them, or maybe just the boldest, watched him hit the water. Then he leapt in after, strong steady strokes pulling toward the point of entry. Diving down when he reached the place where the feathers and bits of broken wing littered the surface of the water, he found the unconscious man right away, not too far beneath the surface at all. The pieces of a wooden framework still wrapped around his torso added to his buoyancy and helped to make him easier to find.

The rescuer grabbed onto the collar of his robe and with one strong pull, brought the unconscious man to the surface. Then he rolled him onto his back with the same grip, placing the face above the water as best he could. Without a pause, he kicked and pulled with the other arm in long steady strokes, until he reached two more villagers that waded out into the water to

The True Story of Icarus

relieve him of his load. Daedalus was dragged through the gentle surf onto the beach, his head placed below his feet and his breathing quickly restored.

As he lay on the beach, his rescuers pulled what remained of the wooden frame away from his chest so that he would be more comfortable. Then they slowly wheeled him back into town on a small donkey cart. Everyone it seemed wanted a chance to look at the flying man. So after arriving at the center of the town, it was decided to care for him right there in the cart, so that everyone could watch him and take turns tending to his needs. They made him as comfortable as they could, wrapping him in soft blankets and treating him like an unresponsive hero. He slept for what remained of that day and night, the villagers keeping a vigil by the cart. When he awoke the next morning, he asked for water and food and hot tea. The people of the town responded with all that they had, bringing the finest fruits and cheeses on the island.

Everyone in the village had a share in the bounty of that morning meal. As Daedalus sat up in the cart, gulping down his tea, replenishing himself, the townspeople began to ask their questions. Daedalus had no choice but to respond and fill in the details. So with the entire town gathered around, he began his new life as a storyteller. And the word began to spread of the man who had flown there from the island kingdom in the south.

And the story passed from Daedalus to the villagers and then to merchants and traders and others who sailed throughout the Mediterranean and it kept spreading, far and wide: the story of an Athenian architect and inventor who built a labyrinth and other fine works for king Minos, but then fell into disfavor and had to flee from the palace with his son, Icarus. To escape their impending imprisonment in the very same labyrinth, they decided to flee from the island. Minos tried to prevent their escape, keeping watch on all the vessels leaving the island, but Daedalus, the inventor, built wings for both of them. Made them from the feathers of seabirds and wax and they were able to successfully leave the island by flying away on the wings.

Daedalus Rising

Daedalus of course, warned his son to fly in the middle passage, between the heat of the sun and the sea below, but young Icarus, enamored of the new found freedom of flight flew too high and the wax on his wings melted and he was lost. So Daedalus flew on alone in his grief to the next island.

The first time that he told it, Daedalus had no idea of just how much, the people would be moved by the power of the words. The islanders demonstrated this, in their decision to change the very name of their island to memorialize the fallen youth. And they did, renaming the island, Ikaria. And to this day if you look on a map of the Aegean Sea, you will see it like a jewel in the blue sea, far to the east of Athens.

And even though he had spoken of returning, Daedalus did not go back to Athens. He found that he enjoyed the storytelling so much, that he traveled around the Mediterranean, moving from port to port and place to place. But even though he did not go geographically back to his original home, to Athens, Daedalus did make his return. He returned to his promise: the one that he made all those years ago in that same city and then expanded on before finally leaving the island in flight, to keep Icarus and his family safe. It was a gift that he gave many times.

And the story slowly and surely made its way through merchants, traders and sailors to the ears of King Minos, who had no reason to doubt any of it. And just as Daedalus planned, Minos never even considered looking for Icarus.

So Daedalus perfected his plan, protecting his son and keeping his son's family safe, right under the nose of the tyrant king. And for all the strength and the might of Minos' army and navy, they were kept at bay by one man living from his deeper purpose, powerless against the words of a simple story. Daedalus had no idea of the power of his words. He never intended that the story Daedalus first told on Ikaria, would survive intact for centuries, long after his grandchildren had any need for its protection.

The True Story of Icarus

So it is finally time for the true story of Daedalus and Icarus to be told. It is time for the world to know that Icarus was not a foolish boy, but a gifted young man with an open heart and a passion for life. Just as it is time to recognize Daedalus' accomplishments, not just as an inventor, but also as a loving and devoted father. Certainly he was the first man to fly on wings of his own creation and some may consider him great for that reason alone. But as he said to Icarus and Sophia before departing from the island, none of it would have happened without the love and loyalty he had for his son. All along his journey, it was the motivation for knowing and following the calling of his heart. Daedalus himself certainly believed that whatever greatness he possessed, came out of that commitment. It was the inspiration for Daedalus to choose to become his own king just as it inspired his own transformation from being a builder in stone and earth and wood, into a builder of wings.

So there comes a time and a turn for each one of us, to find our own voice and to tell our own story to discover and follow our own deeper path and then soar into the light and warmth of the sun.

Epilogue

No bird flies to high on wings of its own making
~William Blake

The mythology of our time in this 21st century, is not so very different from that of our ancestors. They told their stories to their tribes, their communities, to their children and celebrated their histories. The stories have been passed down through the centuries in an unbroken chain. There is great power in these old myths. They are the oral tradition of all people. This book is a retelling of one of those stories.

This book reveals for the first time, the True Story of Icarus, the boy who flew too close to the sun, on wings held together with wax. For far too many centuries, this story has taught lessons about the inevitability of loss and limitation and the reckless folly of youth. It is time to turn away from that old lesson and seek the deeper wisdom. Here, in this new century, it is time to reach for the new lesson, the one that teaches about the power of wisdom and choice, and of the search for meaning through the calling of the heart. To read these words and retell the story, is to reconnect with that ancient chain.

We are not so very different now inside this new century. Each of us is journeying through the experience of life in a human body. We all have experiences of childhood, coming to sexual maturity, the passage from childhood to adulthood, relationship, the search for deeper meaning, the failure of the body and gradual loss of its powers and death. It is a common journey, shared by all. The ancient tradition of telling stories about these life transformations binds us. We share wisdom with our own participation in the timeless tradition of creating our own mythology for future men and women to consider, when they sit around campfires or conference tables and deliberate the course of their lives, the welfare of their communities and the health of the planet.

These are old words, old stories and we are not here to blindly repeat them. They are not law. They are power, nourishment. There is a river of voices coming out of the past, resonating in the telling of the old stories. The river forms an ancient wave, without impediment and true to its own course. This book is part of that flow. To write this book or to read its words is to join in that flow. We are grounded in its power and it is our connection to each other and to the larger universe. Each one of us free to choose to adapt its message into our present moment. Then to mark our own journey, finding our own voice and adding it to the flow of that river, for the next generation to consider.

About the Author

Robert William Case

The author began this life as Bobby, growing up in the heartland in Akron, Ohio. Quickly adapting into Bob, he remained one, long after graduating from high school in the Spring of 1970. That was a few weeks after and just down the road from the shootings at Kent State University, a shocking event in a tumultuous time which eventually instilled a belief, that the culture he had grown up in, had given up the idea of initiating boys into men, or children into adulthood. A few months after that, while listening to two young folk singers in a college coffee house sing their ballad about Icarus flying too high and falling into the sea, he began collecting the first omens and ideas about the Icarus myth, and wondering if initiation as a ritual began losing ground centuries before, when Icarus first fell into the sea and drowned.

Many changes, experiences and accommodations later, to careers and children and marriages, two beautiful children grew into adults, Robert emerged and it was all the perfect motivation and experience for writing this first book, *Daedalus Rising - The true story of Icarus*. Looking back there is much to be grateful for, and knowing that the deepest satisfaction and the best memories come from those times when the heart leads, rather than the head.

Robert is blessed with two grown children. He is a storyteller, a husband, an elder, a marathon runner, a dancer, a writer of poetry and fiction, and practices law in Colorado, where he lives with his wife and their Boston Terriers. He has also appeared in the Boulder International Fringe Festival.

To Learn More About

Daedalus Rising

&

Robert William Case

Robert Case is a speaker and workshop group leader. Additional products, services and contact information are available at the website:

DaedalusRising.com

Robert is available for speaking engagements and personal appearances.

Daedalus Rising

Order Form
Daedalus Rising

$19.95 + 2.50 (S&H)

online at:
http://BooksToBelieveIn.com/DaedalusRising.php

by phone:
have your credit card handy and call:
(303) 794-8888

by fax:
(720) 863-2013

by mail:
send check payable to:
Thornton Publishing, Inc.
17011 Lincoln Ave. #408
Parker, Colorado 80134

If it is temporarily sold out at your favorite bookstore,
have them order more of ISBN: 0-9820838-1-5

Name: _____
Address: _____
_____
Phone: _____
E-mail: _____

Credit Card #: _____
Card Type: _____ Expiration Date: ___/___
Security Code: _____